Barral… of him with his light

While his other hand clenched the Jati, his flashlight picked out a skeleton grinning up at him from the floor. The Nazi uniform rotted onto the bones and the visored officer's hat perched on the skull were grim reminders of the fate of the thousand-year German Reich.

The beam traveled along the floor, until it caught the edge of a round wooden container. A barrel. As the other mercs came up behind him, Barrabas shone the beam around the room. The light revealed a dozen more barrels.

Tom Brown pushed into the room. "The gold!" he shouted. "The—" He stopped and shone his light into one of the barrels. Dark-yellow metal glittered and sparkled.

The gold was everywhere, little flakes and nuggets piled high in the barrels and in small mounds on the floor.

"What the hell!" O'Toole said in surprise. "It's not . . ."

"Yeah. It's not bars or coins," Nanos said slowly. "But what is it?"

Brown lifted a handful of little pieces of gold from one of the barrels. It was old and dull. It looked like it had been chewed. He held the pieces in the palm of his hand.

"Fillings," said Barrabas. "From human teeth. Tons. A hundred million dollars worth."

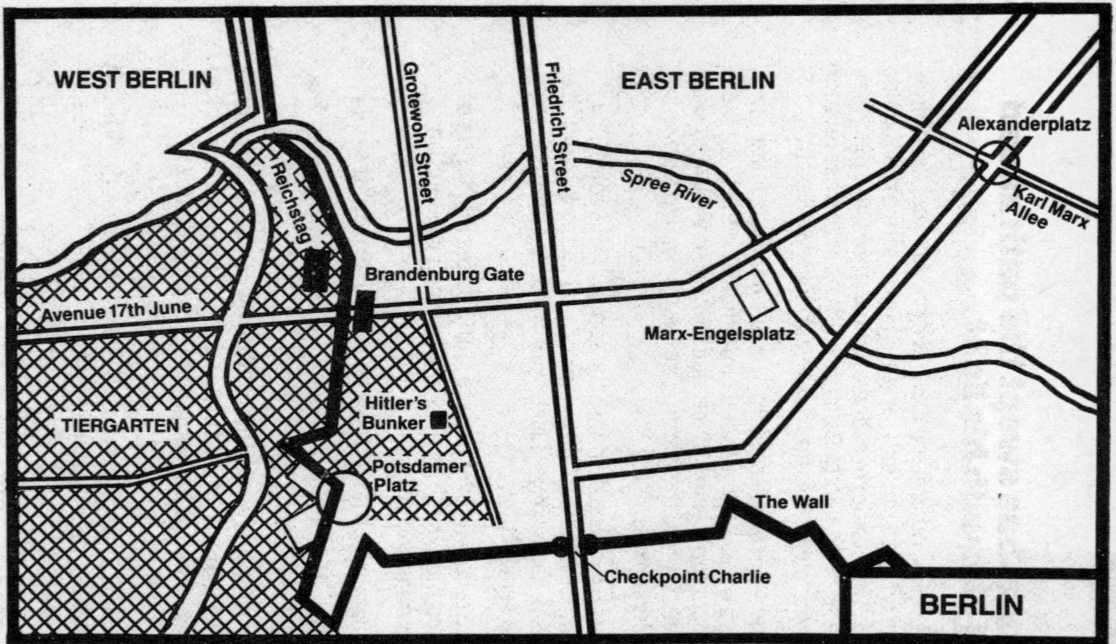
WEST BERLIN
EAST BERLIN
Grotewohl Street
Friedrich Street
Alexanderplatz
Karl Marx Allee
Spree River
Reichstag
Brandenburg Gate
Avenue 17th June
Marx-Engelsplatz
Hitler's Bunker
TIERGARTEN
Potsdamer Platz
The Wall
Checkpoint Charlie
BERLIN

SOBs

AGILE RETRIEVAL

JACK HILD

A GOLD EAGLE BOOK FROM
WORLDWIDE

TORONTO • NEW YORK • LONDON • PARIS
AMSTERDAM • STOCKHOLM • HAMBURG
ATHENS • MILAN • TOKYO • SYDNEY

First edition March 1986

ISBN 0-373-61611-2

Special thanks and acknowledgment to Robin
Hardy for his contributions to this work.

Printed in Canada

1

The classic 1967 turquoise Mustang convertible rolled slowly through the dusty cobblestone streets of Friedrichshagen, a two-hundred-year-old resort suburb on the edge of East Berlin. During the forty years of Communist rule, the elegant old stone cottages had fallen into disrepair. Their ornate stone facades had crumbled and their elaborate wooden trim stayed unpainted. Clouds of summer dust rolled out from under the tires of the car as it bounced over the potholed road until it came to within sight of a lake called Muggelsee.

The driver, a stocky American man, carefully checked for traffic before turning onto the road that ran along the lake. He drove past the beer gardens and outdoor cafés, strung with colored lights, the empty tables waiting for the droves of workers who shortly would be leaving their factories and offices in the nearby industrial districts.

Tom Brown was a thirty-five-year-old American businessman who exported antiques for the masters of East Germany, swapping U.S. dollars for the treasures of their country's heritage. For seven years he had been pillaging Eastern Europe for valuable items to ship back to New York. The nature of his occupation had made it easy for Tom Brown to diversify;

buying and selling was his business. Today, as on any other normal day, he felt relaxed and calm. He always felt that way before doing something extremely dangerous.

The rows of decaying houses of Friedrichshagen ended at an immense Victorian waterworks surrounded by a wrought-iron fence. Beyond it, the pike forest began, struggling up from the sandy soil at the edge of the lake. The American parked the car on the gravel shoulder and got out. It was a bright, hot, summer afternoon. He struggled out of his suit jacket and loosened his tie. Automatically he felt inside the jacket for the leather sheath sewn into the lining just below the sleeve. He disliked guns. But he never went weaponless. Slinging the jacket over his shoulder, he made his way down the path into the forest.

His black oxfords sank into the loose soil and filled with sand. At the bottom of a small hill at the edge of the forest that bordered the lake, he stopped to empty them. Nearby a tall brown metal sign bore the letters FKK. As Brown was retying his shoe, a corpulent middle-aged man and a long-legged blonde with voluptuous breasts strode quietly through the woods hand in hand. They were both stark naked. The American looked up briefly, long enough to notice the woman's bright-red-painted nails. The couple saw him, but didn't give him a second look. FKK stands for *Frei Körper Kultur* or "Free Body Culture." Communist and capitalist, East and West, the German people loved their nude beaches.

Brown retied his shoe and walked along the path to the edge of the lake. Muggelsee, like all the lakes surrounding Berlin, was shallow and muddy. Out on the water, a few windsurfers made use of the scant wind available. Farther down the shore, a grove of willow trees hung over the surface of the lake. Brown walked toward the trees.

He lit a cigarette and waited a few minutes, watching the windsurfers perform their graceful slow-motion water ballet on the lake. Occasionally he turned his head to look through the trees to a nearby wooden shed, identified by a sign that said *Toiletten.* The naked man who he had seen earlier with the blonde entered the shed.

A few minutes later he left.

The American lit another cigarette and smoked half of it. Then, with his shoe, he crushed it in the sand and went to the toilets.

There was one chemical toilet in the small building. The room smelled of urine and disinfectant, but, he thought, like everything else in Germany, it was clean and orderly.

He locked the door carefully and reached behind the flush tank, feeling slowly until he found an envelope taped to the porcelain. He tore it off and sat down. Then he reached into his jacket and pulled a thin dagger from its secret fold. It was ivory handled, the blade long and razor sharp. Set into the butt on each side were two small swastikas. Engraved in the steel blade was a name—SS Captain Ulrich Meser. Brown used the knife to slit open the brown envelope.

The American quickly withdrew a sheaf of folded papers and shuffled through them. They were what he expected—lists of Red Army military supplies at East German army depots throughout the northern regions. They were very impressive lists. At the bottom of the pile was a white envelope. That was for him. He set it aside on the back of the toilet and took out his cigarette lighter.

Working quickly and with a practiced hand, he held the lighter at eye level in one hand and a sheet of paper in the other with his arm outstretched. The lighter doubled as a camera. In little more than a minute he had photographed the papers. Then he refolded them and stuffed them back into the brown envelope.

He retrieved the white envelope, slit it open and pulled a document from it. It was a police report dated 1965. The stamp on it was from the East German secret police, the Staatspolizei or Stapo. The American laughed silently to himself. Ulrich Meser, former captain in Himmler's feared Waffen SS Totenköpfe or Death's Head Division, was not only alive after all these years, he was still living in Germany. A perfect hiding place. So perfect that the Stapo had known his whereabouts for thirty years and couldn't touch him.

Impatient knocks on the door of the shed brought him back to reality. *"Moment Mal!"* he called. Quickly he folded the police report and stuffed everything back into the brown envelope. He pulled a wad of U.S. dollars from his pocket and put it in the envelope with the documents. Then he wedged it behind the pipes behind the toilet.

"Bitte!" It was a woman's voice. It sounded as if she needed to go badly.

He opened the door and stepped outside. It was the blond woman he had seen earlier, still dressed only in bright-red nail polish. The potbellied older man was beside her.

"Entschuldigen," she said, smiling at the American. *"Ich muss urinieren."*

"Bitte." His eyes met those of the man's with a look of guarded recognition as he moved away from the door. The young woman went into the shed and closed the door behind her.

The American walked toward the willow trees without looking at the German man, who strolled nonchalantly after him.

Tom Brown leaned against a tree and lit another cigarette. He gazed out over the lake and blew smoke into the air. The German stood ten feet away with his hands folded behind him.

"It is dangerous to talk, Hermann," Brown said quietly.

"A little, yes," Hermann said softly. "Was that the information you wanted?" Neither man looked at the other.

"Of course. It's all back behind the toilet with the money, so you can return the documents to the *Ministerium* files."

"I meant the police report."

"Yes."

"A curious request. I understand the need for you to have information on army depots. But what does the identity of an old Nazi war criminal who flies outside the power of the law have to do with Western security?"

"None of your business."

Hermann shrugged, as if to say he didn't care. "I trust my senior position in the *Ministerium* will continue to be of use?"

The American dragged slowly on his cigarette and took it away from his mouth.

"Perhaps, Hermann. I don't know right now."

The German seemed disturbed. "But I . . ."

"You need more money? We'll see. Your usefulness to us may have ended. My superiors have asked me to return to New York. Perhaps the operation is finished. I don't know. I will be in touch in the usual way."

The American threw his cigarette into the sand and walked a few paces away. He hated traitors, even when they were useful to him. He especially hated the ones who only did it for the money. Without looking back he walked through the forest and up the hill to his car.

He put his jacket back on before climbing in. The seats were hot from the sun. He sat for a moment at the steering wheel, waging a silent war with a familiar personal enemy. He lost. He dived for the glove compartment and pulled out a small plastic thermos. He unscrewed the cup and filled it with clear cold liquid. Then he reached into the glove compartment again and dug out a little jar of Bulgarian olives. He dropped one into the cup. Vodka martini, dry, straight up.

"To the secret of Nazi gold," he murmured to himself, holding the cup to his lips. He swallowed the martini in a fast gulp.

Then he collapsed back into the seat, relaxed. He could feel his ears burning and his heart thumping. It was always like this, every time he did something dangerous.

It would be only a matter of time before the German and Soviet security services were on to Hermann. Then they would be on to him. It was time to get out. And the agency was calling him back anyway. But finding a hundred million dollars' worth of Nazi gold hidden since the end of the Second World

War would be a nice way to cap a long and honorable career.

Tom Brown rattled the olive in the bottom of his cup and reached for the thermos again. This time he filled the cup half full and sipped.

All he needed was time.

And time was running out.

HERMANN AND HIS BLOND COMPANION crossed and climbed up the hill to a dark green Trabant parked by the side of the road. The Trabant was the pride of the East German automobile industry. It came in five colors and looked like a twenty-year-old Fiat. Unless a person had *"Beziehung"*—connections—there was an eight-year waiting list to acquire a car. Hermann had connections. As a senior officer in an important *Ministerium*, and a high-ranking member of the Communist Party, he was able to get a new Trabant every year.

When they were on the highway and skimming past the big industrial complexes on the southern edge of the city, Hermann turned to the young blond woman.

"Ilsa, my darling. Can you keep a secret?"

"*Ja*, certainly, Hermann." She smiled and tickled him under the chin. He liked that. He smiled at her and removed the wad of American currency from his shirt pocket.

Ilsa's eyes grew big.

"Hermann darling!" She took the money and flipped through it with the edge of her thumb. "Where did you get so much American dollars?"

"Beziehung," he said, giving her the universal explanation for good luck in Communist East Germany. He smiled.

"Ach so," she replied, understanding. She tucked the money into his shirt pocket. Her hand dropped to his chest, rolled over his flabby bureaucratic tummy and crawled down to his crotch. She squeezed. Hermann swallowed and felt a flutter of desire. *Beziehung* could get a man almost anything.

"Come back to my apartment, Hermann dear," Ilsa pleaded, kneading his crotch and wetting her lips with the tip of her tongue.

"Of course, Ilsa." He stepped on the gas.

A few minutes later they pulled into the visitors' parking lot outside a twelve-story apartment building in the center of East Berlin. A forested hill rose up behind it, and a thirty-foot-high red stone statue of Lenin rose up in front. The high rise had been built recently, but the exterior facing tiles had already begun to crack and fall off.

They rode the elevator to the twelfth floor. Hermann grabbed Ilsa by the buttocks and pulled her to him, grinding her pelvis against his. She resisted coyly, pulling away with a mysterious smile.

"Not so fast," she said with a slow wink.

The elevator stopped and they went down the hall to her apartment. Hermann was impressed. It was very big. Much larger than a woman who was merely a secretary in the steno pool at the *Ministerium* would normally have. Wide plate-glass windows opened onto a balcony that looked out over the city. Perhaps she had *Beziehung* of her own. Herman was too horny to care.

"Have a drink, darling," she said, waving toward a liquor cabinet. "I want to change into something more...comfortable." Again that mysterious smile.

She disappeared into the bedroom, closing the door behind her.

Hermann lifted down a small glass from the shelf above the cabinet, admiring the delicate crystal. Definitely *Beziehung,* he thought. Her apartment was almost as well-appointed as his own, and he was the fifth-level senior bureaucrat in the *Ministerium*. He poured a glass of schnapps and gulped it back. Excellent quality schnapps. He felt it bring the blood to his face. The second glass hit him in the stomach along with the sudden desperate realization that something was wrong.

Secretaries from the steno pool were never assigned apartments like this. They shared one-room apartments with their girlfriends until they were married.

Hermann began to sweat.

There was a knock on the door.

"Would you answer that please, darling," Ilsa called to him from the bedroom.

He set down the glass and walked to the door. He looked through the peephole. There was only darkness.

He opened the door.

The two stocky secret policemen pushed into the room, forcing Hermann to back up quickly. One of them slammed the door behind him. Hermann went white with fear. He froze. He tried to call Ilsa. Incoherent sputtering came from his mouth in a spray of fine saliva.

"Ilsanna," he cried finally, his voice stretched thin on a rack of horror. As one of the policemen pulled the brown envelope from his jacket pocket and the wad of currency from his shirt, Hermann heard the bedroom door open. Hard heels clicked smartly on the tile floor.

The policeman spun him around.

"You called," she said.

Ilsa stood ten feet away from him. She had indeed changed into something comfortable—her uniform. The pointed black boots with their thin spiky heels rose to her knees, smoothly hugging the line of her calves. Dark green pants continued along the line of her strong thighs and hips. The shirt bloused out over the black leather belt around her waist, its cross strap rising up between her breasts and over her shoulder. The holster that held the pistol at her side was open. The silver badges on her sleeves marked her as a high-ranking Stapo officer.

She stepped forward slowly and deliberately, snapping her heels on the floor. She was still beautiful Ilsa. But now, her beauty was terrible. Her long red nails had become deadly feral claws, protruding several inches over the ends of her fingers. They were razor sharp.

She shook her blond hair proudly back over her shoulders. Her red lips smiled in contempt.

"Yes, it is me. Ilsa." Her eyes flicked up and down his now-quivering body, filled with hatred. Her mouth twitched. She laughed at him, her eyes riveted to his crotch. "He is pissing himself!"

Hermann suddenly noticed the warm acrid wetness spreading down his legs. The trembling worsened. He couldn't stand. The officers held him up. Ilsa walked forward and took the money and the brown envelope from one of them. She threw the money on the table without a second look. The envelope she tore open with her sharp red nails. Hermann's mouth dropped open, and his breath became ragged and panicky.

"Yes," she said, looking at him. She held one of her hands up and brushed her thumbnail quickly along the nails of her other fingers. There was the sound of metal clicking on metal. She laughed again, long and hard, at the fear and disbelief in his eyes. Then she went back to the contents of the envelope. Her chest heaved and her breath quickened as she shuffled through the papers.

"Some of our most important military secrets, Hermann," she said grimly. "Surely worth more than that!" She picked up the American currency and threw it back down angrily. "And what is this?" She ripped open a white envelope and pulled out the mysterious police report.

She skimmed it, looking at both sides of the paper and then read it carefully.

"Why this?" she demanded, shaking the document at Hermann.

"I don't know! He asked for it. That's all."

She strode over to him and stretched her arm back, threateningly. Hermann struggled, but the two beefy policemen held him firmly. Ilsa slammed him across the face with the flat of her hand. Then she pulled her hand away slowly. The razor-sharp metal nails sliced smooth lines down Hermann's face. Warm blood spilled from the lacerations and dripped down his neck.

Hermann screamed.

"I don't know! I asked him! He refused to say. Only that he wanted police information on this... this war criminal named Ulrich Meser."

Ilsa backed off, regarding him suspiciously.

She looked at the two secret policemen. "Get rid of him." She jerked her head toward the glass doors to the balcony.

Hermann screamed again.

The two burly men dragged him across the room. He tried to dig his heels into the thick carpet. They lifted him and carried him over the doorsill to the balcony. Hermann opened his mouth to scream again. One of the security men balled his fist and smashed him in the mouth. Instead of words, the bureaucrat sputtered blood and broken teeth. The policemen changed position; each now held Hermann by a shoulder and the seat of his pants. They lifted him over the railing. An ugly rasping sound escaped from his mushed-up mouth as Hermann drew one last sobbing breath.

They chucked him over.

Hermann sailed from the balcony like a bird taking flight on outstretched wings. The rasping blossomed to a high-pitched scream as the body plummeted to the earth twelve stories below.

The policemen went back inside.

"Too bad," said Ilsa, still studying the police report on Ulrich Meser.

The sound of a crash came through the open glass doors. Ilsa looked up briefly in that direction; falling bodies had a way of obstructing traffic. She turned to the two agents.

"I want to know why the American spy needed this information. So, all our plans must be changed. We must get hold of Fritz and tell him to stop."

The two men exchanged worried glances.

"It may be too late," one of them said.

"Stop him!" Ilsa shrieked, raising her hand and spreading her deadly fingers. "Stop him now! Before the American spy is dead!"

2

Liam O'Toole stretched his neck in the stiffly starched collar of the white shirt he wore and flexed his shoulders inside the tuxedo jacket. He was nervous. The organ music that flooded the church with saccharine tones made him even more nervous. He had never been married before.

Alex Nanos leaned over and whispered in his ear, "What's a matter, O'Toole, you look nervous?"

"I'm scared, Alex. What am I doing here?"

"Getting married, Liam," Nate Beck explained matter-of-factly from the other side. Nanos and Beck, the two capricious cohorts in crimes against the female species, were best men at the wedding of Liam O'Toole, the second man in charge of the Soldiers of Barrabas. It was a rare occasion—O'Toole was completely at their mercy. Usually it was the other way around.

"Haven't you ever been scared before?" Nanos asked.

"Sure. On my way into battle."

"Well, there you go, Liam. The difference between this battle and the other kind is only in your choice of weapons."

"Well said, Alex," Nate Beck commented with some degree of admiration. Alex Nanos was known for brawn not brain. The tuxedo-rental people had had a hard time finding a suit to contain the Greek's bulging biceps and wide pecs. As it was, the suit barely fit, and the soldier's musculature stretched the fabric away from the studs that held his shirt together.

O'Toole eyed them dubiously. "You guys are a big help." His Adam's apple bulged against the stiff collar as he spoke. He felt like the collar was shrinking, strangling him like a formal, rented garotte. He stretched his arms and pulled the silly ruffled sleeves out beyond the cuffs of his jacket, and then he looked down to survey his body.

At six feet and two hundred pounds of muscles, Liam O'Toole hadn't been an easy man to fit, either. His preferred apparel was nothing at all, and that was usually what he and Susy Doyle wore around the house. What had begun as a casual encounter with a hot New Jersey housewife had turned rapidly into love. The love of his life. Six months later they were still doing it two or three times a day, and when Susy said she wanted to tie the knot, O'Toole decided to walk right down the aisle. He never thought it would happen to him.

But it was about to.

So here he was, waiting for Susy to arrive at the front door of the church and join him at the altar. Suddenly a chilling thought entered his mind and he looked at Alex Nanos, panic written across his big Irish face.

"What if she doesn't come?"

Nanos threw him a wink and tapped him on the shoulder lightly with his fist.

"Then it's back to being a bachelor and living the high life again, old buddy," he answered mercilessly.

"Don't sweat, Liam," Nate cut in. "She'll be here."

O'Toole smoothed his thick copper-colored hair back and stuck a finger inside his shirt collar to stretch it. "I can't stand this much longer," he muttered.

"Amazing what a guy has to do to get laid," Nanos said, sighing.

O'Toole looked at him murderously. His hand turned into a fist and his arm stiffened. Beck nudged him. "Hold it, Sarge, we're in church."

Nanos put on an innocent expresion. "Hey, O'Toole," he asked, "when do I get another chance to rib you without getting a fist in the face?"

"Never," O'Toole said, deadly earnest.

Alex Nanos smiled a mouthful of white pearlies.

While O'Toole grimaced bravely and endured the banter from Nanos and Beck, the small audience, gathered to watch the nuptials, waited patiently. On one side of the aisle sat the friends of the bride—about thirty nice, polite suburban people, mostly women in pretty flowered dresses with white gloves.

O'Toole's buddies were seated in one row in the other side of the aisle. Claude Hayes sat on the outside. Next to him Geoff Bishop sat beside Lee Hatton. Then came Billy Starfoot II. The SOBs were all there—except for the colonel. Barrabas was on the invitation list, but none of the mercenaries knew where he was, what he was doing or how to get hold of him. It was often like that between wars. This wasn't the first time their leader had just disappeared. But this time, when Claude Hayes, Lee Hatton and Alex Nanos had returned from a successful mission in South Africa, they carried rumors that the colonel was having girlfriend problems. O'Toole had called Erika Dykstra, the girlfriend in question, in Amsterdam. She said she didn't know where Barrabas was, hadn't seen him and didn't have any plans to change that. That didn't sound good. There was no question that being a professional soldier was hard on relationships. That was why O'Toole was seriously thinking of giving it up. He hadn't mentioned that to anyone yet. When he made the decision, the colonel would be the first to know.

In the audience, on the groom's side of the aisle, Billy Two sat with his eyes closed, rocking on the seat. He hummed quietly until Bishop slammed his elbow sharply into his side. Billy stopped the humming but continued to rock with his eyes closed. The full-blooded Osage Indian was a great guy, but ever since he'd endured a torture session with GRU, the Russian military police, he hadn't been quite right.

"What's he doing?" Lee Hatton whispered in Bishop's ear. Her short-sleeved white dress with the low neck set off her short dark hair and deeply tanned skin. It was the first time most of the mercenaries had seen her dressed that way, and her appearance in front of the little church had brought a chorus of whistles that made even Geoff Bishop break into a smile. It was an open secret that she and Bishop were lovers.

He whispered back to her. "Billy said he was going to go into a trance to find out why the colonel isn't here and where he is."

"Oh dear. It's really too bad he didn't show up."

Claude Hayes leaned over from the aisle seat. "Did I hear you say the colonel's coming?"

Lee shook her head. "Uh-uh. Just the opposite. No one could track him down."

"Not even Erika?"

"Uh-uh." Lee looked at Bishop and turned back to Hayes. "I don't think he and Erika are..."

"Ah." Hayes nodded and straightened up in his seat. "So it happened. Well, knowing the colonel, he'll turn up when he gets it out of his system. It's just too bad he couldn't be here to see this. He and Liam go all the way back to Vietnam."

"It's ironic, isn't it," said Lee. "Liam finds it just when the colonel and Erika..." She left off, nothing more to say.

Hayes nodded silently.

On the other side of Lee, Billy Two suddenly jerked upright, causing Bishop to turn to him.

"What's happening, Billy Two?"

The Osage warrior opened his eyes slowly and pivoted his head sideways to look at the Canadian pilot.

"Colonel Barrabas will not come. He is far away, and he is alone. He wants to be alone. He will not come to any of us for a long time."

Bishop's brow furrowed and he looked puzzled. "How do you know that?"

Billy Two looked at him without blinking. "I know," he sighed. "But I know you do not believe me, either."

Bishop shrugged and smiled in spite of himself. "I don't disbelieve you, either, Billy. Let's just say..."

Suddenly the organ music erupted into the familiar opening of "The Wedding March." The spectators rose to their feet. Nanos slipped down the side aisle and took his place beside the bride at the entrance to the church.

The love of Liam O'Toole's life was outlined against a radiant burst of sunlight. She stood in a simple white dress, holding a bouquet of flowers and looking positively virginal. She slipped her arm through Alex Nanos's and started up the aisle. Her eyes were riveted to the eyes of the man she was to marry.

In the front row Lee nudged Geoff Bishop. "Look at Liam. Have you ever seen anyone so happy?"

Bishop looked. The big, blustering, red-haired Irish-American ex-sargeant and Vietnam veteran, who had led him and the other SOBs in everything from bar brawls to bloody battles, looked like he was about to ascend to heaven.

Outside the little stucco church, someone else observed the happy occasion from behind the dark gray windows of an expensive Audi. Walker "the Fixer" Jessup watched O'Toole's girlfriend enter the church and heard the organ music flood into the street.

Jessup sighed and slapped his enormous thighs in frustration. Damn it if he didn't always have the dirty work to do.

He pulled a small thin notebook from his suit pocket and flipped it open. His people had filled him in on the honeymoon plans. O'Toole and his new wife were due in Miami in a few hours for an extended stay in a luxury hotel. O'Toole could afford it. He'd made a bundle working for Barrabas. Jessup knew all about that. Barrabas worked for the Fixer and the Fixer worked for the pols in Washington.

Right now they had another job, a serious one involving a recalcitrant spy named Tom Brown. There was only one person with enough guts to do it for them.

Nile Barrabas.

Walker Jessup was the only person in the world who knew where he was.

And Liam O'Toole was probably the only person in the world who could get through to him.

The Fixer glanced at his watch and scratched the day's growth of stubble on his chin. Then he wiped his eyes. He'd been up all night in his New York office studying the files, going through telexes and putting queries out on the computer network. The word on Barrabas's whereabouts had come in only an hour before.

O'Toole. He needed O'Toole.

But for the time being Barrabas could cool off. Another twenty-four hours would probably do him good.

But it was going to be a helluva honeymoon for the newlyweds.

3

It was almost ten when O'Toole awoke. The hot Florida sun was beating in through the hotel windows and the open door to the balcony. They were on the twentieth floor, so all he could see outside was the deep blue sky. He could hear the ocean waves washing up on the sandy beach below.

Beside him, Susy stirred, clutching at him tightly. She pressed her face against his chest, and he could feel her leg moving under the sheet to rest between his. Then he felt her mouth open and her warm wet tongue against his skin. She was awake. She was tempting him. It had been like this from the beginning. O'Toole sighed with ecstasy and pulled her to him.

Barely had they finished when a soft buzz and flashing red light on the telephone by the bed alerted them to a message from the desk.

O'Toole reached over and answered it. "Hello."

The man at the other end spoke with the grim propriety of a hotel desk clerk. "Sir, there is a gentleman here at the desk who wishes to speak to you."

O'Toole pulled himself up in bed, slightly stunned by the news. The only people who knew where he was were his fellow mercenaries. So who was at the desk? Susy smiled and rolled toward him, wrapping her arms around his naked waist.

"Who is it, Liam?"

O'Toole cupped his hand over the receiver. "Why don't you grab a shower, Susy. Then we'll have breakfast." He winked at her. She gazed up at him, with big blue sexy eyes.

"Okay." She threw back the covers. O'Toole watched as she walked to the bathroom. He wanted her all over again. It had been that way for six months now and showed no signs of stopping. He put the telephone back to his ear.

"Hello."

"Sir."

"Who is it?"

"He wouldn't leave a name, sir."

"Describe him."

"I beg your pardon?"

"Tell me what he looks like."

"Well, sir," the desk clerk spoke softly now, "he's about medium height, quite a large man, and his suit is a little rumpled. In a hurry, I'd say."

A large man. Not a tall white-haired man. Not Barrabas. "You mean a fat man," O'Toole said.

The desk clerk coughed uncomfortably. "Ah, you might say that, sir."

The Fixer. What the hell was he doing here. O'Toole cast his eyes in the direction of the bathroom. He could hear the shower. Damn, it was his honeymoon. And if it was a mission, why wasn't Barrabas here. Unless something had happened to Barrabas. The worst part of it was that Susy didn't even know what O'Toole did for a living, didn't know he was a professional soldier, a mercenary. She thought he sold agricultural machinery. This was not just a bad thing to happen to a honeymoon. It was a disastrous way to start a marriage. O'Toole resolved on the spot to do something he'd been thinking about doing for a while now. Quitting.

"Tell the gentleman to meet me by the pool in ten minutes." He hung up. "Susy!" He sat on the bed and called to her. He heard her turn the shower off. The glass doors slid open.

"Who was that on the phone?" she called through the half-closed door. She was drying herself.

"A business call. I have to go downstairs and take care of it. I'll meet you in half an hour in the restaurant. We'll have brunch."

He reached for his clothes and started dressing.

Ten minutes later he walked through the hotel lobby, past the stalwart tourists in Bermuda shorts and straw hats forming a straggly line to await the tour bus. He crossed the lobby and descended steps that led to the courtyard pool. The sunlight was blinding. He felt in his shirt pocket for his sunglasses, but they weren't there. He squinted and searched through the landscape of baking brown bodies. The monumental Texan known as the Fixer was as obvious and uncomfortable as a dry-docked hippo.

Jessup sat in a lounge chair at the far end of the pool. His mirrored sunglasses shielded his gaze, but his head moved back and forth as he systematically inspected rows of seminude females, basted and broiling in the tropical sun. In contrast to the frieze of worshippers of the almighty tan, captured and reflected in his sunglasses, Jessup wore his tie knotted tightly at his neck, and he kept his suit jacket on. As O'Toole came closer he made out the stains down the front of Jessup's shirt and his wrinkled pants. He looked like he'd slept in the clothes he was wearing. For about a week.

The Fixer jumped when O'Toole pulled out the lounge chair beside him and sat down. He had been focusing intently on a brown-skinned beauty walking the other way.

"Howdy, Jessup." O'Toole fixed the Fixer with an icy stare. Jessup's face was white, but his nose and cheeks had already taken on a pinkish tinge from the sun. It wasn't O'Toole's problem. He hadn't invited Jessup to Miami.

"Liam, good to, er, see you! Congratulations on—"

"Jessup, you didn't come here for that. I may as well tell you now. Right up front. I'm quitting. I wanted the colonel to be the first to know it. But I have the feeling I should tell *you* right now."

Jessup glanced around the courtyard, not looking at anything in particular. He reached over to the table beside him where a pitcher of lime juice sweated. He poured a tall glass, letting the ice cubes plunk heavily, and handed it to O'Toole. Then Jessup filled his own glass.

"What about the money?" The Texan slurped slowly and thoughtfully on his drink. He set the glass down and reached into his pocket for a once-white handkerchief and mopped his forehead.

"I don't need the money. Half-a-dozen missions with the colonel made me a millionaire. It's made all of us millionaires. That's not the reason any of us keep working. You gotta have other reasons for work like that."

"Like what?"

"Like wanting to live your life on the edge of nothing," O'Toole answered, suddenly angry. "Not caring if you live or die as long as there's another fight somewhere, when you can take stock of everything in the world that pisses you off and make the bad guys pay for it. That's what keeps us doing it, Jessup. Or, at least some of us."

"So what's changed?"

"I'm married. And there are two things that don't go together—mercenaries and wives. I made my choice." O'Toole set his glass down and started to get up.

Jessup's hand went out. "Wait!"

O'Toole paused, half out of his chair.

"Wait a few more seconds. Hear me out. It's all I ask. Just listen. After that it's up to you."

O'Toole looked at Jessup for a moment. Then he sat down reluctantly. Jessup's entreaties were the thin edge of the wedge. The Texan wasn't known as the Fixer for nothing. The ex-CIA agent was skilled in the fine art of manipulation.

"What do you think it'll take to change my mind, Jessup?"

"Barrabas."

O'Toole shook his head. "Uh-uh." He looked pensive. He rubbed his hand against his chin. He hadn't shaved. He hadn't even brushed his teeth. "Jessup, I grew up in a big family. Twelve kids. I was the oldest. We lived in the slums of Belfast. I was a fighter by the age of ten, and when I was sixteen I was running bombs for the IRA. I got out of that and came to America where I volunteered for the army and Vietnam. There wasn't much of a war left, what with Vietnamization going on and the great pull out. But I met the colonel there. I was with him when he rescued those airmen from Karl Haupt and the heroin smugglers. Barrabas was more than just another officer. He was a leader. A guy we'd follow to hell and back. Just the way he was . . . it was vibes. That's what some guy from California used to say. The colonel had vibes. You could trust him. So when you put together this covert-action team and Barrabas picked me for the number-two spot, I went for it. You know what my life's been since I left the army? Booze and females. And you know something, Jessup?"

O'Toole leaned forward in his chair and looked at the Fixer. He couldn't tell what the fat man was thinking behind the shades.

Jessup shook his head.

"I thought Barrabas's offer—to join this covert-action team to fight dirty secret wars for you guys who pull the strings in Washington—I thought that was the answer."

Jessup waited for O'Toole to go on, but the Irishman was finished.

"You stopped drinking whenever you were with the colonel on assignment. You always hated civilian life."

O'Toole nodded. "That's right. Going out with the colonel is a real high, Jessup. A real high."

"So what's the problem?"

"You come down, Jessup. You always come down. And man, you have to pay for those highs with lows like you can't imagine. You don't know where I've been between wars, Jessup." O'Toole covered his face with his hands and wiped his eyes. "You know my pa died when I was young, and my ma disowned me because of what I did for the IRA. My brothers and sisters think I'm dead. And you know something else?

Susy's my high now. The lows are gone. I'm married. We want to have a family. A little house with a white picket fence." O'Toole laughed and shook his head. "I never thought I'd hear myself say that."

He looked at Jessup.

The Texan sat motionless, a large, conspicuous chameleon on a rock.

After a long silence the Fixer finally spoke.

"A friend of the colonel's is in serious trouble."

"So tell the colonel."

This time it was Jessup's turn to look away.

"Can't do that right now."

"Why not?"

Jessup seemed to be studying the bikini-clad beauties diving into the blue waters of the pool. He picked up his glass and drank nervously. Then he mopped his forehead again with the handkerchief.

When he finally spoke, his voice was low and dark and he spoke not to O'Toole but to the empty space in front of him.

"He's hit a low." Jessup drank quickly, emptying his glass.

O'Toole waited. Jessup said nothing.

"What kind of low?" O'Toole's voice was as quiet as Jessup's.

The Fixer shifted his vast bulk uncomfortably in his chair. "Opposite of yours," he said. "Erika left him. For good."

O'Toole turned away, whistling to express his total surprise. Barrabas and Erika always seemed pretty solid together.

Jessup went on. "Y'see, I know the price you pay. And what he pays, too. How many friends did you have at your wedding, Liam? Just the SOBs, right?

Your fellow soldiers. Because you don't have any other friends. Not really. Not like everyone else."

O'Toole nodded slowly, agreeing reluctantly.

"Not in this line of business," Jessup continued. "Maybe all of you think it's because you're tough and you don't need friends. Or you tell yourselves it's because you'll get them in trouble if you talk too much some night over a bottle of booze, or that someone trying to take a shot at you will get them instead. Maybe it's because you don't want to get close to anyone and then get killed and leave them crying. Or else it's the other way around. You're loners. Every last one of you. You all go out chasing after wars because you can't get close to people."

This time it was O'Toole's turn to shift uncomfortably in his chair. There was a lot of truth in what Jessup was saying. But Christ, why did the man have to say it out loud. O'Toole used to drown thoughts like that in a fifth of whiskey.

"And Barrabas?" he asked Jessup, hoping to get him back on point.

"Barrabas has got no one. Not even Erika. And he's hurting inside real bad. The problem is that he doesn't even know it. I got a job for him to get his mind off losing his girlfriend. But someone's got to talk him into doing it." Jessup removed his sunglasses and looked O'Toole directly in the eyes. "Liam, you're the oldest friend he has. And you're the only one who can do it."

"Where is he?"

"He went berserk."

Just then O'Toole felt two soft hands cover his eyes. A woman's voice, almost giggling, asked, "Guess who?"

"No contest." O'Toole smiled, putting his hands up to feel hers. "I bet it's Susy-Q."

She laughed and took her hands away, bending over to kiss him as she came around and sat on the end of the lounge chair. "You're late for brunch in the restaurant, darling." She was wearing a bikini. He felt her breasts heavy against his chest as she leaned over to kiss him.

"Oh, baby. I'm sorry. I really am." He motioned to the Fixer. "This here's a business colleague, Walker Jessup. Walker, this is my wife, Susy Doyle."

"I'm truly sorry, ma'am," said Jessup in his dress-up Texas drawl as he shook her hand, "to interrupt this special time for you and your new husband."

Susy looked at Liam. "Business?" she asked.

"Sort of." He looked at the Fixer. "A friend of ours, a business friend, is in trouble. Personal things."

"And I'm afraid your husband is his oldest and dearest friend, ma'am, and the only person who can talk him out of a most dee-structive course of behavior."

Jessup the Fixer was fixing again. He put his sunglasses back on and resisted the smile of satisfaction he felt for a job well done.

Susy turned to Liam O'Toole. "But if that's the case, darling, you should go and help him!"

"But we... you... it's our honey—"

"I know, darling." She grabbed his hand and held it tightly. "But your friends are important, too. If this person is having a personal crisis and needs you, then I want you to go." She looked at him earnestly.

O'Toole returned the stare and made the decision he had wanted to make, thankful for his wife, who, he thought, must be the most incredible woman in the world for leaving him the room to make it. He turned to Jessup.

"This is the only person who could ever change my mind."

The corners of Jessup's mouth twitched. The smile could be concealed no longer. The Fixer reached inside the jacket of his crumpled suit and withdrew an airline ticket from the pocket. He handed it to O'Toole, who was too stunned to say anything.

He looked at Susy. She laughed and rumpled his hair.

"You take care of this, then we'll continue our vacation," she said with a wink, briefly poking the tip of her tongue against her upper lip, forcing O'Toole to smile. The index finger of her right hand was straying down his chest. He gulped. She knew all the tricks. She was incredible. While it still astonished him, he had no doubts that he was in love.

"Where is he?" he asked, again turning to Jessup.

The Fixer stood up, straightening his suit as he prepared to leave. "In Amsterdam. In jail."

4

Nile Barrabas looked up as the diffused morning light filtered through the bars of the window in his jail cell. Outside, low gray clouds rolled over the Dutch sky and pressed down on the earth. They were always there. It rained off and on. He knew because tiny drops would sometimes sting the glass, leaving watery tracers to drip along the panes. Amsterdam was three meters under water. Three damned meters. Almost ten feet.

Or it would have been if he had succeeded in what he had set out to do, he thought, scratching his head, wondering if it really had been such a good idea. His hand strayed a bit too far back on his head and hit the soft part near the enormous raw lump. He winced as the unseen steel hand squeezed his cranium again and pain washed through his brain.

He remained perfectly still. Gradually the agony subsided. If he moved very slowly, it would be all right. He opened his eyes.

The big high-ceilinged cell was painted white. The cement floor was gray and its coldness seeped up through his bones. There were bars on his windows, painted white, but there were no bars on the cell. Instead, a white metal door with a tiny window led out. The door was securely locked. He knew. He'd already tried it.

But then, he had figured, what the hell. So I break out. Where do I go next? It was then that he realized he didn't really care. Squatting in the corner of the cell between the narrow prison bed and the barred window was as good a place to be as any.

Something else occurred to him. He pushed himself slowly up from the floor and looked out the window. He was on the second floor of a building. If he had succeeded yesterday, the water would be halfway up the wall of his cell. He shook his head. Bloody Dutch. Built half their country underwater. They even had a saying here, God made the world but the Dutch made Holland.

The only thing that kept the ocean from their door steps were the dikes, those long, thin man-made mounds of earth along the coasts and rivers.

A jolt of pain kicked through his head again. He grabbed his forehead to stop it from splitting open. He sat down quickly and kept perfectly still again. The pain ebbed. He tried to remember the details of how he got there.

It had started two days earlier, when he had arrived in Amsterdam, checked into the American hotel and phoned Erika. They talked. Erika wouldn't promise anything except to talk again in a few hours. In the second conversation she told him there was no way. It was over, she said, and there was no going back.

"Don't you think that's something you should tell me in person?" he said. She agreed to meet him at a coffee shop near the flower market. It turned into a big scene. A major motion picture. They were yelling at each other across the table while frantic waiters tried to hush them and indignant diners harrumphed loudly at their tables. Finally Erika threw a heavy water tumbler.

Nile ducked.

A good thing, too, because if it had hit him it might have taken his head off. Erika, the beautiful, svelte blond woman who was the softest, gentlest creature on the earth, threw it with such force that it whizzed past the eyebrows of the people at the next table, sailed through the plate-glass window and, amid a cascade of breaking glass, smashed into the fender of a tan Volkswagen bearing German license plates parked at the curb outside, leaving a sizable dent.

Barrabas threw some money on the table, grabbed her by the hand, and they ran for it. They got outside just as a plump German with a tiny mustache reached his car. They braved the gauntlet of his vile Teutonic curses with long-aproned waiters from the café right on their heels.

They ran until they were breathless, Erika leading Nile through the narrow sixteenth-century streets in the older sections of the city, along canals and over bridges until they lost their pursuers. Then they turned and looked at each other and burst into hysterical laughter.

Their eyes met, shared the joke and for those mad minutes were together again. Nile stopped laughing. He looked at her, raised his hand and touched her on the chin just below the full line of her mouth.

She turned away from him.

"No, Nile." She shook her head, and then her eyes met his. "No."

She turned around and walked away.

He watched her grow smaller down the long cobblestone street, until it curved away and she turned and disappeared. She never looked back.

He went back to the hotel. Tormented, he fell into a blind, dead sleep.

In the morning he phoned her.

When she said no again, he... Barrabas swallowed and flicked his eyes around the stark white jail cell. He didn't want to admit it but it was true. He had pleaded. He had begged.

"Please, Erika, please. Let's just talk some more. Let's meet in the café downstairs. I promise to behave, Erika. I swear..."

All along Erika kept saying no, she couldn't take it anymore, waiting around for him to finish a war and then never knowing when he might have to take off again. Or whether he'd come back each time. No, she said. Nothing was going to change her mind. But finally she agreed to meet for coffee.

He went at the appointed time and waited for hours. He memorized every detail of the art deco interior of the elegant European café, watched the grandes dames come and go, the intellectuals reading their newspapers, the American tourists come to gawk. He figured out how he and the SOBs would launch an assault on the café if terrorists ever holed up there with a room full of hostages.

He played out the entire battle in his mind's eye. At the end of it, the American café was a ruin, the hostages were free and the terrorists were just so much meat.

He thought about everything but the fact that Erika had stood him up.

Cut the crap, he thought, looking around the jail cell and wondering if there was a way out other than the door. It was a knee-jerk response; he had it every time he found himself in a prison cell. And he had always found the alternative exit.

The crap, he thought again. He had sat there in that café with nothing on his mind except Erika. She wouldn't leave him. She couldn't. It was unthinkable.

He went back up to his hotel room and phoned her again. He didn't expect her to answer, but after three rings, he heard Erika's sultry hello. It made his heart stop and fall like a piece of stone into his stomach before booming back into commission. His voice was dry. Something was squeezing his guts.

"Erika. It's Nile. I waited for you..."

"Didn't you get my message?" she asked evenly.

"No, I..."

"Well, get this one." Click.

Click. Kuh-lick.

He knew he was going to hear that sound for the rest of his life. Kuh-lick. She had hung up on him.

Nothing like this had ever happened to him before. Nothing like Erika or the way she was leaving. He didn't go berserk right away. That came later, after he had gone through a couple of bottles of that wretched Dutch Genever at 170 proof. Barrabas had wandered blind drunk through the streets of Amsterdam until he found himself in the red-light district, where a long-legged hooker called to him in heavily accented English, "What ya doing tonight, darling?"

The answer came to him right out of the blue.

"I'm going to drown this fucking city," he told her. "I'm going to wash the whole rat-infested mess away."

She kept smiling at him. She didn't know what he was talking about.

He threw her a crooked smile to let her know he meant it. Well, he thought, feeling the cold penetrate up from the hard cement floor of the cell. It had seemed like a good idea at the time. He closed his eyes, dimly aware of the steady raw pain from the big swollen bruise at the back of his head.

A metallic click alerted him to someone's entry. He allowed one eyelid to flutter up just enough to see who it was—a young guard in a stiff, badly cut uniform and long stringy yellow hair.

"Mr. Barrabas!"

So they had finally discovered who he was. How, he wondered. He'd been picked up without ID and so far had resisted speaking to anyone. But police were the same everywhere. They had ways of finding out.

"*Ja*, we know who you are. Follow, please. You have visitors."

He thought for a moment about who it might be. State Department, maybe. U.S. Consulate? Erika? He knew it wasn't her but hope dies hard.

The guard waited patiently at the door.

He stood up and tripped as the blood rushed to his head, and pain blackened his vision. He put his hand out to the wall to steady himself until he could see again. The guard made no offer of assistance.

When the pain in his head dropped back to its normal level, he went for the door. The guard stood aside and Barrabas walked into the corridor. It was stark and white and brightly lit by bulbs under little metal cages high in the ceiling. Metal doors similar to the one that led into his cell lined the walls. Another guard and a matronly woman in a uniform, her hair pulled tightly back into a bun, waited for him. She looked at him sternly, but her eyes were filled with concern. She had the look of a liberal who believed in rehabilitation over retribution.

Barrabas winked at her. It made her look more sad. Obviously Barrabas was going to require more rehabilitating than the usual case.

"Mr. Barrabas, you have some visitors from your country," she said in perfect English. The two male guards continued to look reproachful. The woman saw him as fodder for correction, but he was nothing more than a dangerous criminal to them.

Barrabas smiled at them.

"Lead on!" he commanded. It was time to face the music.

The last thing he was ready for when the guard opened the door to the visitor's room was the fat smiling face of Walker Jessup. He sat at a table with his hands folded in front of him, trying to look sympathetic.

Barrabas did an about-turn and bumped into the solid figure of the matron, who blocked the doorway like an antitank column, her arms folded across her ample chest.

"Mr. Barrabas," she scolded him, "Mr. Jessup and Mr. O'Toole have come all the way from America to see you."

Barrabas nodded. "You don't say."

He turned around. This time he noticed the man standing next to Jessup. Liam O'Toole. The big red-haired Irish American started to smile and stepped toward the colonel. Barrabas put his hands up in the stop sign. He pulled out the chair across from Jessup and sat. O'Toole sat down, too.

The guards left and the matron closed the door behind her. The silence was as cold and stark as the room.

Jessup broke it.

"Sometimes I think the world is full of assholes," he drawled in his finest Texan.

"Yup," Barrabas nodded, agreeing. "One for every man, woman and child."

O'Toole put his elbows on the table and his face in his hands. "Sheeesh," he groaned. It was getting off to a bad start.

Barrabas and Jessup looked at him. O'Toole straightened up, looked at the colonel and burst out laughing. He leaned back, rocking on the back legs of the chair, and slapped his knee.

"Colonel, did you know you caused more damage to the dikes of Holland than anyone has since 1945, when the Germans bombed them on their way out?" He threw his head back and laughed some more. "Jessup!" He waved his hand at the Texan. "Get out the bloody bottle!"

Smiling, Jessup pulled a fifth of cheap whiskey from his inside jacket pocket along with three metal cups.

Barrabas started smiling, too—a sort of silly, sheepish half smile because he was doing it in spite of himself. But he had to admit, if anyone could get through to him it was going to be these two clowns.

"Drink?" Jessup asked as he poured and set the cup in front of Barrabas. He poured one for himself and O'Toole and spilled almost as much on his suit. Then he set the bottle in the middle of the table.

Barrabas's two friends raised their drinks and threw them back. Barrabas watched. Then he picked up the bottle from the center of the table, put it to his lips and sucked back the booze.

Jessup and O'Toole watched the whiskey disappear from the bottle with a swirl of gurgling air bubbles. The empty bottle popped when he took it away from his mouth. He slammed it back down on the table. His head felt a helluva lot better.

The Fixer smiled and reached in the other side of his suit jacket. He pulled out a second fifth of whiskey. This time it was the expensive stuff. He filled his glass and Liam O'Toole's. Barrabas's was still full.

The colonel nodded. He had to hand it to the Fixer for being on top of things. Jessup set the bottle down and held his hand around his cup to warm the whiskey.

"So tell us, Nile. What was it like?" Jessup laughed.

"Wellll," Barrabas started slowly, staring at the glass of whiskey in front of him. "I guess it was a pretty dumb thing to do."

"Yeah, but what was it like?" O'Toole urged, genuinely curious.

Barrabas looked at him briefly, then stared off into space trying to remember. "I knew the exact place to go because I'd driven up there once—up in Hagensvoort where they built new dikes to drain the Zuider Zee and turn it into farmland. There was all this earthmoving equipment. I remember getting out there somehow..."

"You stole a car," Jessup told him.

"Ah." The recollection was dim. "Well, when I got up there, I found that hot-wiring a bulldozer is no sweat if you know how to do a tank or a personnel carrier, and any grunt can do that. So I just drove it up the dike and started digging." He picked up the glass of whiskey and threw it back.

"They say that in another five minutes you'd have breached the dike," O'Toole told him, filling his glass from the bottle. "The first small waterfall over the earthworks would have washed the soil away until it became a torrent. The dikes would have disappeared like brown sugar in water. You're in all the papers. Headline news. 'Unidentified American goes berserk.' There've been riots outside the U.S. Consulate."

"The fun part was when they came after me," Barrabas continued. "By this time the top of the dike was pretty torn up and, me, I'm riding high in the dozer. All of a sudden the hill's crawling with all these cops, waving their hands at me to stop and running after me. So I turned around and chased them with the dozer, waving the big shovel at their asses." He burst out laughing, then stopped just as quickly. "It was such a dumb thing to do," he added morosely.

O'Toole shrugged. "If it was Los Angeles, they would have shot you."

"Yeah. Hear they just knocked me out. Some cop got up on the back of the dozer, I guess. All I know is that the lights went out and I woke up here."

They were all silent for a minute, none of them looking at the others, each waiting for someone else to talk first. O'Toole's knee was jumping like crazy. It always did in tense situations where he was forced to be idle.

Barrabas sensed the discomfort of his comrades. "So," he said. "What bring you guys here?"

O'Toole answered, rocking back on the legs of the chair again and waving his hand in the air. "Hey, a guy's in trouble. What do you expect from friends? For us to forget about you?"

"Yeah well, I sure as hell wasn't thinking about anyone else," Barrabas said.

"Nile, I've got a job I think will interest you," Jessup said finally. "Take your mind off things."

"Yeah right. I was waiting for that," Barrabas said coldly. "I knew this wasn't just a social call."

"Oh. Well..." Jessup shrugged. "If you're not ready..."

"What do you mean?"

"No, no!" The Fixer waved his hands dismissively. "It's probably better that you don't do it. If your mind's not totally on the job, it'd be dangerous for you." He skipped a beat. "And for everyone else."

Barrabas stared across the table at the Fixer. He wanted to kill the man. Now.

"Damn you, Jessup!" He stood up, knocking his chair back, and dived for the Texan's neck.

"Colonel! Colonel!" O'Toole jumped in, calmly grabbing Barrabas's arms and pushing him gently to his side of the table. Jessup whitened and pushed his own chair back a foot. Barrabas's eyes were still on him.

"It concerns an old friend of yours, Nile," Jessup said evenly.

O'Toole pulled Barrabas's chair upright and kept talking as he coaxed the colonel to sit. "It's like what friends do for friends. Like us coming to see you, Colonel. That's all."

"Who?" Barrabas sat down.

"Remember Tom Brown?" Jessup asked him.

Barrabas nodded. "Tom was CIA. I knew him when I was with MAC in Saigon and later in Washington. He's crazy."

"Yup," Jessup agreed. "But who's not? Anyway, he's in deep trouble."

"What?"

"He's been in the cold for several years now. As an American businessman buying art treasures and stuff from the German Democratic Republic. And on the side he's been passing on photographs of Russian military documents given to him by a high-ranking government official. It's been a successful operation, but it had to be wound down fast. Section D, Counterintelligence, found out his cover was blown, and he's apparently marked for liquidation. They ordered him out, but he won't come."

"He won't come in?"

"Nope. He refuses to. And won't say why. He could be killed any time. And the CIA doesn't want to lose him. He's high-class talent."

"Bullshit, Jessup. They're afraid he's a double agent and that the liquidation story is a cover-up. Or that he's turned over. And they want me to find out."

"Well," O'Toole broke in, "it sounds to me like it'd be better for this Tom Brown if you run into him before someone else does."

"Is that what you want, Jessup?"

The Fixer nodded.

"So, where's he now?"

"East Berlin. At the Palast Hotel. As far as we know, he hasn't left."

"I'm going with you," O'Toole said.

Barrabas smiled, ready to shake on it. Then he remembered. "You got married? When?"

"Yesterday, Colonel."

"Oh shit." Barrabas felt terrible. "I'm sorry. I forgot, Liam. I'm real sorry."

"Colonel!" O'Toole laughed. "Don't be sorry. It was the greatest day of my life."

The two mercs shook hands, and then Barrabas slapped him on the shoulder. "Congratulations!"

"Wait'll you meet her, Colonel."

Then Barrabas's face clouded. He shook his head. "No, Liam. No, you're not going. You should be with your wife right now, not with me out there somewhere fighting whatever it is this time."

"Colonel, it's okay. Susy and I talked it over. She said go. And we'll be together when it's all over."

Barrabas kept shaking his head, not wanting to hear what O'Toole was saying. He'd heard himself say it too many times already. About Erika and him.

"Don't you see, Liam. That's what's happened to me and Erika. There's not a woman alive who thinks she can't handle it. But they're wrong. They can't. Oh, they go on for a while acting like everything's all right. But really it's too much for them. And when you think about it, they're right. It's not fair." He kept very still and looked his buddy straight in the eye. "Fighting's a drug, Liam. Every mission is the hit and if you get out alive it's cause to celebrate—to go for another hit. It's a gamble. Take your chances. Do you live or die? We're crazy. No one can live with that."

Barrabas shrugged and thought a moment about his own words. "Sometimes I don't know how we live with it. I've seen it happen, in the eyes of guys I knew when I fought in the mercenaries' wars in Africa. They'd come back one time and their eyes looked tired and dead. Next time they went out they wouldn't come back. I wonder if, sometimes, soldiers just get tired of winning."

"Nile," Jessup called softly to him from across the table. His eyes met the big man's. "You sure you want to do this?" This time, the question was straight.

"You can't stop me now, Jessup." Barrabas gave him a toothy smile of defiance. "Look here!" He jabbed his finger toward his own sharp blue eyes. They sparked. Anticipation.

"Colonel, I'm coming. Because—" O'Toole groped for words "—I believe you got a lot to say about it, and I've been doing a lot of thinking about our line of work. Now I'm married, so I gotta talk it out. I'm coming this time, Colonel, because it might be the last." Their eyes met over the table.

Barrabas nodded. He understood.

"So, let's get out of here," was all he said.

5

As Nile Barrabas was walking out of a Dutch jail with Liam O'Toole and Walker Jessup, American CIA agent Tom Brown was parking his car in a no-parking zone on Leipzigerstrasse in East Berlin, near the front doors of a windowless stone warehouse.

He tapped on the heavy oak doors. A moment later he heard the clanking of the locks and the door swung inward. A young German man greeted him enthusiastically.

"*Guten Tag*, Herr Brown! Everything has been done as you have instructed, and we are ready."

Brown stepped into the cool, musty interior. Low-wattage light bulbs spaced along heavy beams in the ceiling illuminated dozens of large wooden packing cases with excelsior spilling out of their tops.

"Very good, Bruno," Brown slapped the young man on the back as the door closed behind him. Bruno smiled, obviously pleased that he had done the job well. He had been assigned to Brown as an assistant by the East German exporting agency and had proved to be a good worker. He handed Brown a clipboard holding a sheaf of papers and with a pen tied to it.

"You have only to make the final inspection and the boxes will be sealed."

Brown moved forward into the warehouse, peering into the tops of the crates and glancing down the list. He flipped through it quickly.

Ornately carved chair backs and the surfaces of polished marquetry tables showed through the mounds of wood shavings. He had no desire to play antique dealer any longer. It had been an excellent cover, but its utility was over. The morning papers had carried the story of a high-up bureaucrat's suicidal plunge from the balcony of a twelfth-floor apartment. The Stapo had got to Hermann. He would be next if he didn't move quickly. He initialed the bottom of each page and handed the clipboard back to Bruno. The young man looked perplexed.

"But, Herr Brown, you did not look in each of the—"

"Don't be so German, Bruno," the American laughed. "I trust you to make sure that it's all *in Ordnung*. What about the trunk I asked you not to pack up?"

"This way, Herr Brown." Bruno led him through the maze of packing crates toward a glass-partitioned office near the back of the warehouse. An old wooden chest, heavily scarred with the wear of years, sat near an empty crate and a mound of packing material. Brown removed a key from his pocket and bent to unlock it. He saw the look on Bruno's face. He could read it like a billboard.

"Have you opened this chest and looked inside?" he asked.

Bruno shifted uncomfortably. He stammered, not wanting to admit it.

"It must have frightened you," Brown said, giving the young man a break. He threw back the lid of the chest. The smell of mothballs drifted out. At the bottom, a single item was laid out neatly—a ceremonial SS uniform complete with insignia, ribbons and medals. The leather sheath at the belt was empty.

"It is very dangerous to possess such things in Germany today," Bruno said nervously.

"Dangerous anywhere," Brown mused. "The chest had come with a load of furniture from Dresden a few months ago. The uniform was in it. It belonged to a war criminal named Ulrich Meser. His name was engraved on the back of the medals."

"You will take this to America?" Bruno asked.

Brown shook his head. The Nazi regime had been the most evil in the history of mankind. He wanted nothing to do with that kind of gruesome memorabilia. He reached into the chest and started to roll the uniform into a ball. "No. I'm going to throw it in the river."

Bruno nodded with satisfaction. It was obvious he felt this was the best solution. "And this war criminal," he asked, "what happened to him?"

Brown continued to roll the uniform without answering. "Hand me some twine," he asked his assistant. When Brown had discovered the uniform, he had used his contacts with the Nazi Documentation Center in West Berlin to trace Ulrich Meser's history. The SS captain was reported to have been killed in action in Berlin in the last days of the war. But the chest had contained more than a uniform. There were old identity papers, citations and notebooks, all pertaining to the life and career of Captain Ulrich Meser during the war, bearing his writing and his signature.

Several notebooks were unusual. They contained observations on the weather over a period of several years, and some kind of numerical code that even a cryptologist friend at CIA headquarters in Langley had been unable to decipher. The notebooks were clearly written in Meser's hand. But they dated from the 1970s. Ten years ago, the SS captain was still alive. It had only taken a little digging in the dung heap of recent German history to learn the terrible secret that Meser had allegedly taken with him to the grave—the secret location of a hundred million dollars' worth of Nazi gold, hidden in Berlin as the Russian army swept through the suburbs toward Hitler's bunker.

He took the twine from Bruno and started wrapping one end around the rolled-up uniform. "He's dead," he finally answered. "He was killed in April 1945, not far from here."

"You know a great deal about this man," Bruno commented.

Brown looked at him as he tied the knot. Bruno was a bright young man. He probably had to make regular reports to the Stapo on Brown's activities. He shoved the uniform into the German youth's hands.

"You have the rest of the day off," Brown said. "Throw this in the back of my car on your way out."

Bruno slapped his forehead with the heel of his hand in the universal gesture that meant "Boy, am I a dummy."

"Herr Brown. *Entschuldigen bitte!* I completely forgot. The New York office telephoned for you."

Brown stood up and took a billfold from his suit pocket. He peeled off an American fifty-dollar bill.

"It's illegal for me to give this to you," he said, pushing it into Brunos's shirt pocket. "But I don't think you will tell anyone."

The young German's eyes lit up. Fifty American dollars was worth ten times that much in purchasing power in his country.

"Herr Brown!"

"It's nothing, really. Go enjoy yourself. Buy something for your girlfriend." Brown went into the glass office, where an old telephone sat amidst papers on a dusty desk. He lifted the receiver and wiped it on his pants before putting it to his ear. It left a dirty mark. Bruno started toward the front of the warehouse. Brown stuck his head outside the glass partition and shouted. "Are the doors locked?"

Bruno turned around to yell back. "*Ja!* Front and back." He waved goodbye and disappeared outside. The door locked automatically behind him. Brown dialed the operator and asked to be connected to New York. He heard the line click and hum with static and the faraway sound of German voices talking on the crisscross of communications lines. The circuit breakers for the lights were on the wall beside his head. While he waited he snapped them off, leaving only one line of lights burning from the office up a narrow aisle piled high with crates to the front door. The rest of the warehouse was dark.

Finally the telephone rang in New York. It was answered on the second ring. A woman's voice.

"Anglo-German Importers. Can I help you?"

"Tom Brown in Berlin, Ruth. You called?"

"The boss has asked me to instruct you to return to New York with the next complete shipment."

Brown gripped the receiver. They wanted the microfilm of Hermann's documents, and they wanted him to bring it in person. It was confirmed now. They were calling him in.

"The shipment is going out the usual way, Ruth." He meant it was in a secret dead drop, to be picked up by another agent. Damn, he thought, why did they have to call him in now?

"We have a tight budget situation here, Tom," Ruth told him. "Your instructions are to proceed to the New York office immediately as a cost-saving measure."

Brown nodded to himself, finally understanding what they were getting at. It was more than just the termination of his assignment. His cover was blown. They wanted him out before the other side eliminated him.

"You'll find everything in order, Ruth. I'm taking a vacation. I worked for it. I earned it." He hung up before she could respond and sat heavily in the rickety chair next to the desk. He wanted a drink. He thought about the thermos in the glove compartment of his car. He imagined the taste of an ice-cold vodka martini. There was nothing like life's little pleasures to get the mind off major problems. Like what to do next.

As he sat, he saw the light in the warehouse momentarily brighten, as if a surge of electric current had gone through the wires. He stood up and left the office, heading for the thermos in the glove compartment of his car. As he turned up the aisle that ran through the crates, shivers cracked his spine as though icy fingers had slipped around the back of his neck.

The metal door at the back of the warehouse revealed a thin line of lights from outside. It wasn't closed properly. It wasn't locked.

It had been no surge of current in the wires that had momentarily brightened the light. Someone had surreptitiously opened the back door.

Someone was inside.

Looking for him.

He ducked.

He barely heard the whispered pop of the silenced gun, but he caught the spray of splinters as the bullet chewed into a wooden crate just above his head. It was fired from the far corner of the warehouse, beyond the back entrance. Brown went down on his hands and knees, crawling quickly and silently into the office. The lower half of the partition was wood and afforded some protection. Other than that he had only one slim advantage over the man with the gun.

He was in familiar territory. The gunman was not.

There was a metal coatrack in the corner. He grabbed it at the base and tilted it toward the circuit breakers, pressing one of the hooks against the last switch. The long coatrack was heavy and awkward. It slipped past the switches and crashed forward, smashing through one of the glass windows of the office partition. A nerve-jangling shatter of broken glass echoed through the silent warehouse. He hoisted the coatrack back up and listened. Very faint, but not far away, he heard footsteps.

He tilted the coat rack again, digging the blunt end of one of the hooks in against the switch. Slowly he applied pressure, squeezing his hands tighter around the base and edging it against the switch. It didn't move. He leaned his weight slowly forward. The angle and length of the coatrack gave him virtually no leverage.

Then he felt it move. Straining not to relax his weight, he pushed slightly.

The switch closed with a jerk, plunging the warehouse into total darkness. The coatrack slid forward and fell through the broken window, knocking out more pieces of glass.

The rest of the glass windows around the office began to explode, hailing shards of glass. Brown hunched into a corner, pulling his head down with his hands as a torrent of jagged glass rained down on him. He dug inside his jacket and pulled the Nazi dagger from its sheath. He put it on the floor beside him. Then he pulled a handkerchief from his breast pocket. He tied it around his hand and knotted it, leaving his fingers free. He unknotted his tie and tore it off, wrapping it around the other hand. He picked up the dagger and put it between his teeth.

Making as much noise as he could, he ran for the door of the office, then deked left and threw himself into the corner just as his assailants fired again. The bullets pinged into the concrete floor, sending a shower of dust and sparks into the air. The muzzle-flash was near the back door. The killer had a straight line of vision into the office. Brown felt like the last pin in a bowling alley at the end of a tie game.

He groped gingerly along the edge of the partition above him, where jagged pieces of glass lined the sill. Jump high, he told himself.

He picked up an old newspaper from the top of the desk and rolled it slowly and silently. Then he pulled out his lighter and cocked it. He held it close to the newspaper, hunching his body around the flame so that no light would be seen. The newspaper caught.

It burned quickly. He drew his body away as the flames licked up the dry folds of the paper toward his hand. He tossed it out the office door.

The makeshift torch threw wild shadows across the walls and ceiling as it arced into an open crate.

The gunman fired again.

Chunka, chunka! Bullets smashed into the doorframe and office furniture. Brown grabbed the edge of the windowsill above him and jumped, kicking his legs up high and swinging them over.

Sharp pieces of glass stabbed through the fabric over his palms, piercing his skin. There was no time to consider the pain.

The flames from the newspaper had spread to the excelsior. They gulped greedily at the highly flammable material and rose higher, lighting up the other side of the partition, landing on his feet. He grabbed the dagger from his mouth and ran straight down the aisle between the packing crates toward the front door.

At the end of the row of crates, he stopped and climbed upon one, stepping up to the lid of another. The front doors were barely ten feet away. He knelt on the crate and looked over the top of another one. He waited.

The fire spread quickly, blocking the back door. Already flames were licking at the wooden beams overhead near the rear of the building. The air filled with acrid smoke. His eyes watered.

Brown waited.

The killer came.

He was big, and his face was ugly. But there was no confidence in his eyes. He moved now like one bent on escape, not on pursuit, running along the far wall of the warehouse away from the flames.

The back of the old warehouse was a wall of fire, flames leaping from crate to crate and sweeping toward the front of the building. The fire was building to a loud roar.

Brown wiped his eyes and followed the killer from his hiding place behind the crate. The smoke was growing thicker. The killer was disoriented now, almost in a panic.

Panic was the killer's greatest enemy.

The man with the gun turned from side to side, looking mainly for an exit through the maze of crates, but also for the American spy he was sent to liquidate. He spun around and fired at a noise behind him.

But it was just the fire, leaping and running, crawling along the floor and up the hills, hungry for the dry dusty wood of the ancient building. The killer ran.

He swerved low around a row of crates and fell into the center aisle on his hands and knees. The crate behind him burst into flames.

Brown waited. He unwrapped the handkerchief from his hand. It was wet with his own blood, and an ugly wound gaped across his palm. He held the sticky cloth to his nose and breathed through it to filter the smoke. The fire was only twenty feet away now and coming fast.

The killer staggered down the aisle toward the front door. By now, his only thought was escape from the conflagration that threatened to roast him alive. He threw himself at the front door and fumbled with the locks. There were three of them. He undid the first and grabbed the second.

Brown wiped his eyes. His throat was raw from smoke inhalation and his lungs were heavy inside his chest as he desperately suppressed a cough.

The killer had the second lock open.

The American waited. He sucked air through the bloody handkerchief.

The third lock was undone. The killer pulled at the heavy door with both hands, holding his gun at a useless angle. Slowly the door swung open.

Brown jumped.

He fell savagely on the big man's back, grabbing the man's forehead with one hand and covering the man's eyes. The killer leaned back, bellowing with anger and surprise. Brown wrapped his leg around the killer's knees, immobilizing him. The big German assassin lost his balance as Brown's dagger pierced sideways through the middle of his neck.

Brown yanked it forward. The dagger sliced through the killer's neck, opening up his throat.

The man's head tilted back, and the spinal cord dislocated with a crunch. Blood from the severed jugular hosed ten feet out the open door. Brown dropped the body and jumped out of the way as it crashed to the floor. The crates nearest the door burst into flames, which stretched hungrily to the ceiling.

Tom Brown pulled the door open. The dead man's eyes were still open, but they were dead eyes. The spurts of blood pumping through the open neck diminished as the heart stopped beating. A piece of burning timber fell from the ceiling across the dead man's chest. His clothing started to burn.

Brown pushed through the door into the blinding sunlight of the street.

Shouts and the sound of running feet greeted him. Workers were rushing from warehouses farther down the street and racing toward the fire. A distant siren grew louder.

He rushed for his car, jumping over the door into the front seat and dropping the bloody dagger on the seat beside him. The ivory handle was sticky and red.

Brown started the car and squealed into the street, turning off Leipzigerstrasse into the traffic heading toward the city center. He wiped his mouth with the sleeve of his jacket. It was covered with blood. With one hand on the wheel, his foot pressing the accelerator and the tires squealing as he turned corners, he zigzagged through side streets and reached for the thermos in the glove compartment. He spun the cap off and drank long and deep, slowing his car to merge into the traffic along Frankfurter Allee.

The sounds of the sirens faded. He pulled into a side street and stopped the car. Brown drank deeply from the thermos and felt the vodka and vermouth rush into his veins. He felt better. He poured some of the mixture on his face and began to wipe the blood off. The vodka stung and turned pink.

The situation wasn't good.

His cover was blown. His agency wanted him to come in from the cold. If he went now, he could get out safely. If he didn't go, the agency would withdraw all support and leave him to fend for himself. That was the rule. In the meantime the Stapo had sent their killer dogs.

All this when he was on the verge of discovering the hiding place of a hundred million dollars' worth of legendary Nazi gold.

He was all alone.

And he'd just run out of time.

6

Not far from where Tom Brown mulled over his situation, and yet a world away, in the American sector on the other side of the Berlin Wall, another man was thinking about the Nazi gold. Ernst Krankenkor drew the curtains across the windows of his apartment in the old neighborhood of Kreuzberg.

In the dark room, he fumbled in his pocket for matches, found them and struck one. The match sizzled to life, throwing sudden shadows up on the walls. Herr Krankenkor moved to a sideboard, shielding the match with his hand to keep it from blowing out. Deftly he lit two candles.

The wicks sputtered slightly before burning smoothly and cast an even mellow light in the room. Krankenkor reached over the center of the sideboard to the thick velvet curtains that hung against the wall. He thrust them aside. The giant portrait of Adolf Hitler smiled serenely down at him. But the dead Führer's eyes looked beyond Krankenkor to some distant vision of a Nazi future, to the ultimate triumph of the fatherland, to final victory—that which had eluded him when, in defeat, he had put a bullet through his brain in the Chancellery bunker on April 30, 1945.

Krankenor stepped back and stood rigidly at attention. He snapped his heels sharply together and flung his right arm stiff and straight into the air at a forty-five-degree angle to his body.

"Sieg heil!" he cried, not as loudly as he would have liked. In modern Germany, where the money-bag democrats hold power, one had to be cautious in one's allegiance to the fatherland.

Krankenkor's arm dropped and he held his pose a few seconds longer. Then he swung around and goose-stepped softly on rubber heels across the room to an ornate armoire.

He grasped the handles on the mirrored doors and ceremoniously swung them open. Inside, catching the yellow glow from the candles, his uniform hung above a pair of tall black boots, swinging slightly on its hanger and beckoning him like a mysterious enchanter.

He stripped and donned pants, then shirt, buttoning the collar with its gold SS studs, and tightening the brown leather belt at his waist and across his chest. He sat to pull the boots on. They felt good. With each item of the uniform, his breath quickened and he felt mystically charged with an iron will.

He stood up, his heavy boots clunking on the floor. They made him taller, prouder. His uniform excited him. He wanted to do it with a woman dressed like this, if only it was not so dangerous, so illegal in Germany. In the real world, Ernst Krankenkor was nothing more than a balding middle-aged German who ran a corner *Kneipe* in the poorer part of town.

Behind closed doors, in the privacy of his apartment, he was a someone. He was a leader. *Sturmbannführer* of the Bitburg Patriotic Group.

And a double agent.

Each month he received from the German government a check for several thousand marks for his work as an informer for the Verfassungschutz, the German version of the FBI. The money financed the work of the Bitburg Group. In exchange he pretended to act as an infiltrated agent working undercover in the outlawed neo-Nazi movement.

He supplied the Verfassungschutz with information on weekend outings where neo-Nazis learned how to use weapons, and in particular he told his Verfassungschutz bosses about the Group's efforts to distribute leaflets proclaiming "Hitler is the future," and their plan to resurrect the banned Nazi newspaper *Volkischer Beobachter*.

Harmless information.

It was nothing compared to their real plans. They had already bombed installations belonging to the American army of occupation and a train station in Hannover. Future targets included installations along the border with East Germany, not to mention trains from Holland and Poland, countries that imprisoned Nazi heroes under the twisted rubric "war criminals."

Hitler was the future. The goal of the Bitburg Group was to rebuild the thousand-year Reich and nothing less. That would take money—a great deal of it. Much more than he received from the Verfassungschutz in exchange for a few pieces of feeble information.

Money was on its way, however. A plan had been formed and had been put into operation this very day.

He closed the doors of the armoire and observed himself in the mirror, throwing his shoulders back and standing erect. There was one thing missing.

He went to the sideboard and from a drawer withdrew an arm band. It was blood red, emblazoned with a white circle and a left-handed swastika, the symbol of the Nazi Party and the thousand-year Reich. He slipped it on. Now his uniform was complete. The ritual was finished. He felt strong. Determined.

He felt like Adolf Hitler.

The doorbell rang.

Sturmbannführer Krankenkor left the room and walked down the long narrow corridor that led to the front door of his apartment. He peered through the tiny peephole.

A tall elderly man in an expensive blue suit, white shirt and tie waited in the hallway, leaning slightly to one side and supporting himself with a polished wood cane. A fedora was pulled down low over his eyes, throwing his face into shadow.

It was Horst von Blutliebe. Under another name, he was one of the most powerful civil servants in the country. But he had other interests.

Krankenkor stood back and unchained the night lock. He opened the door, standing carefully behind it so his uniform could not be seen from the hallway. Von Blutliebe looked around, as if unsure that he was not being watched.

He stepped furtively into the dark hallway of the apartment.

Krankenkor closed the door behind him and double-locked it.

"Straight down the corridor," he said. "Toward the light."

The elderly gentleman removed his fedora, revealing a full head of snow-white hair. Even in the darkness, his eyes shone like radiant chunks of blue ice. He looked at Krankenkor's uniform doubtfully, then turned and strolled slowly up the hallway, his cane tapping on the floor ahead of him with each step.

"Why must you wear that ridiculous uniform, Herr Krankenkor?" he asked, entering the room where the candlelit portrait of Adolf Hitler gazed beatifically into space. He pulled his kid gloves off, finger by finger, and threw them into his hat, which he set on the sideboard beside his cane. He spun around to face Krankenkor.

"It seems to me that you yourself wore a uniform like this forty years ago," Krankenkor said bitterly. Von Blutliebe sometimes treated him as a buffoon, the same as the desk jobbers and the gray eminences of the Verfassungschutz office. He resented it. He was, after all, *Sturmbannführer* of the Bitburg Group. A someone.

"Endlich bist du jemand," von Blutliebe said, as if reading Krankenkor's mind. "At last you are finally someone." But the man who had once been the third-highest-ranking SS leader in Nazi Germany said it with a bemused smile, with sarcasm.

"Ja," said Krankenkor defensively. "That's right. And were you not also someone once?"

Von Blutliebe glanced down at his finely manicured nails. "*Ja.* At the time our uniforms were, how shall we say, the height of fashion. But, at the time, our armies controlled all of Europe. And Berlin was still—" he grasped for words, as though betrayed by the pain of the memory "—still had not been..."

"Bombed? Reduced to rubble?" Krankenkor finished the sentence for him. "Our leader was betrayed by the German people, whose spirit had been weakened by Jewish and Communist infiltration." He gazed reverently at the portrait of the *Führer.*

"Enough," von Blutliebe said a little sharply. "It is sufficient to say that we need a dictator once again."

"Fatherland, we are coming!" Krankenkor spoke not to the elderly Nazi, but to the portrait on the wall, his voice rising in adulation.

"And speaking of coming," von Blutliebe said wearily, ignoring Krankenkor's display of reverence to the dead dictator, "has our guest arrived?"

"Not yet."

As Krankenkor spoke the words, the doorbell sounded. Krankenkor smiled and left the room. Von Blutliebe heard the door open and the sound of two sets of footsteps in the corridor.

The man who came into the room with Krankenkor was about forty and wore a dark trenchcoat, wet from the rain. His hair was dark brown and clipped short, and a wet strand was plastered to his forehead much like Hitler's.

But this man was no Hitler. His features were sharp, with a small pointed nose and prominent chin. He was of medium build, neither muscled, fat nor thin, and his shoulders were hunched; his small brown eyes darted in their sockets like the eyes of a rat sizing up an infant for dinner. He had the appearance of being both pursued and driven.

He carried a heavy, expensive valise, almost a meter long, which he set on the floor. Von Blutliebe and the newcomer eyed each other silently.

"May I introduce our American friend." Krankenkor smiled at the elderly Nazi, who gave a curt nod of his head.

The American extended his hand. The corners of his lips twitched as he forced a smile. "Haupt. Karl Haupt. At your service."

"Indeed." Von Blutliebe shook the proffered hand briefly. It was clammy and soft, yet somehow reminiscent of the talon of a bird of prey. As an opponent, he would be formidable, and devious. "Haupt. That is a German name."

"My ancestors were German immigrants to America."

"Ach so." Von Blutliebe nodded, turning to the portrait of Hitler on the wall. "Our *Führer* said to me once that America is a mutt race, polluted by niggers and Jews."

Haupt stiffened, considering his reply.

Von Blutliebe continued. "That was only his opinion. But look what happened to him. In the end your country triumphed over ours."

Krankenkor's mouth dropped open in shock at von Blutliebe's words.

The elderly man looked him square in the eyes. "I knew him, as a personal friend. You did not, Herr Krankenkor."

The *Sturmbannführer* closed his mouth and narrowed his eyes suspiciously at the former SS leader. The older man was becoming distracted and began to pace rapidly.

"Hitler was a genius who turned into a fool. He became obsessed with his power. He thought he was infallible, that it was impossible for him to make a mistake. He thought the great Germanic gods were riding with him as his armies marched across the face of Europe. Then he decided to attack Russia. Many of us tried to warn him, but he listened to no one."

Von Blutliebe stopped and looked sharply at Haupt and Krankenkor. "These mistakes must never be made again," he said. "We need a dictator, not a madman."

"Some people might say the two things amount to the same," Haupt said slowly. Something amused him. It showed in his eyes. It annoyed both the Germans.

"Let's get down to business," the American continued. "All that you've told me so far is that there's a hundred million dollars' worth of Nazi gold hidden somewhere and that a tenth of it is mine if I help you get it. Ten million dollars."

"Yes. All the money we need to rebuild the German Reich," Krankenkor hissed. "Hitler's legacy to us. To the fatherland."

Von Blutliebe ignored him. "During the war I was the commander of an elite squadron of storm troopers, Mr. Haupt. We were responsible for eastern security of the Reich, a harrowing task that involved, of course, the summary executions of... many people." He paused and examined his fingernails. "I was of good Prussian family, early supporters of the Nazi Party. Thus, as the Red Army closed in on Poland, the *Führer* called me to his bunker on one of his rare visits to bomb-shattered Berlin. *Ja*, Berlin. Once the most beautiful city of Europe, you know. The night I arrived was the second night of continuous bombing runs from your Air Force, Mr. Haupt. Berlin burned. The city of my youth was little more than glowing piles of charred rubble. I swore I would avenge its destruction."

Von Blutliebe's fist clenched savagely as the terrible memories ripped through him. He looked off into space, as if he saw ahead of him not the room, the burning candles, the portrait of Hitler or his two conspirators, but the blackened ruins of the burning Nazi capital.

"Go on," Haupt urged him softly, with a little smile.

Von Blutliebe returned to reality. He looked at Haupt, his icy eyes flashing with anger. "My *Führer* gave me that opportunity to avenge the defeat of war and in the future, when the time was ripe, to rebuild the Third Reich. Those were his very words to me, Mr. Haupt, 'when the time is ripe.'"

"And this opportunity involves stockpiles of gold?" Haupt guessed, walking closer to the elderly Nazi with his head cocked to one side. He watched the German's face with dark shiny eyes.

"Yes!" Von Blutliebe arched his eyebrows, "Yes! Millions of dollars' worth of gold was to be moved from Poland to a hiding place of my choice."

"So where is it?" Haupt demanded.

"I don't know."

The room was silent for a moment. Von Blutliebe looked down, then paced slightly before resuming. "I assigned five men to do the job. They had to work quickly, to find a place to hide the gold and then to ship it to that place. One man, Ulrich Meser, was in charge. A very responsible SS captain, he was to report to me when the gold was hidden. I had other more pressing matters to engage in at the time."

"Such as making sure your escape route was ready and identity papers forged," Krankenkor said accusingly.

"It was important that I survive," von Blutliebe shouted angrily. "That I go underground, because

I...I..." His face reddened. "I was the one...the *Führer* choose me as his heir. It was to me that he entrusted the task of rebuilding the Reich!" His outburst ended with a spluttering cough. He banged himself on his chest and fell back against the sideboard, pausing to catch his breath. Slowly he continued.

"I took the identity of a prominent concentration-camp inmate and had him gassed," he explained. "Baron von Blutliebe was reported killed in action. I even arranged for a body to be found. Under my new name I entered the ranks of the new democracy. Baah," he said in disgust, "now I am a prominent member of the civil service and my work is indispensable to the welfare of this fraudulent country. I serve the vassals and bootblacks in Bonn."

"You serve the *Führer*," Krankenkor reasured him. "As I do. I lead the Bitburg Patriotic Group. But without you, Herr von Blutliebe—" the *Sturmbannführer* held his hands out imploringly "—the fatherland would have no future."

"The gold," Haupt interjected, trying to get them back to business. "What use is it if you don't know where it is?"

"It was transported from Poland to Germany, and it was hidden," the old Nazi SS leader said softly, his voice showing signs of sadness and defeat. "But events got ahead of us. The Russians on one side. The Americans on the other. It was so bad that in Berlin you could ride from the Eastern front to the Western front on the subway. Captain Meser was on his way to report to me in my hiding place when he and his four men were killed by a land mine. The hiding place of the gold died with them."

"So?"

Von Blutliebe whispered conspiratorially. "He left a map." The old man's eyes lit up, burning again with the vision of victory. "For forty years the map has been waiting in American hands, without them even knowing that they have it!"

"Where?" Haupt asked eagerly.

Von Blutliebe turned. This time it was he who gazed up at the portrait of Hitler, his eyes glowing in reverence. "In Berlin." He looked at Haupt. "In the Nazi Documentation Center, the archive that houses the records of the Nazi Party, which were seized by the American army in 1945."

Von Blutliebe picked up his fedora from the sideboard behind him and tipped the gloves out. "It remains only for us to liberate it. Then the gold will be ours. It will be necessary for us to force our way in, of course, since the Documentation Center is still controlled by the American army of occupation. Have you brought...?" His eyes fell to the black valise that Haupt had carried in.

Wordlessly, Haupt bent over and grabbed the handles of the valise. He hoisted it up and carried it to a table, where he unlocked the clasp on one side and pulled the zipper down. After rummaging through the top of the valise, he pulled out a long heavy object wrapped in cloth. He tore away the fabric. The yellow light of the candles gleamed dully on gun metal. He tossed the submachine gun in his hands, a slight smile creasing his sharp features, and held it out for Von Blutliebe and Krankenkor to see.

"Beautiful!" said von Blutliebe, genuinely impressed. He walked over to Haupt and took the weapon from his hands. "Never have I thought I would be able to hold again the MP40 *Maschinenpistole* in my own hands."

"I have five here," said Haupt. "And plenty of the special 32-round mags of 9 mm parabellum that I have had specially manufactured, since they are no longer officially made."

"You see, Herr Krankenkor, what a beautiful gun we made," the old SS commander said to the neo-Nazi leader. "This was the first submachine gun ever designed entirely of plastic and metal, with no heavy wood butt. It weighs barely four kilos and fires five hundred rounds per minute. It was so popular that in the last days of the war we captured many Allied soldiers who preferred this gun to their own."

Krankenkor reached out and took the gun from von Blutliebe, stroking the barrel and nestling it in the crook of his elbow to test its heft. "I have heard the legends of this gun," he said. "The Schmeisser!"

"Yes," von Blutliebe affirmed. "That's what it was called. Although Hugo Schmeisser—he was a close personal friend of mine—did not design it. It was merely manufactured in his factories. More than a million were made. Today they are almost impossible to find. I must congratulate you, Mr. Haupt." He nodded at the American.

Haupt coughed slightly. "There is the matter of payment."

"Of course." Von Blutliebe reached inside his suit and pulled a thick wad of deutsche marks from his pocket. "Thirty thousand deutsche marks—ten thousand dollars." He threw it on the table near the valise. "Just the beginning, Herr Haupt."

At that moment a soft tapping sounded on the front door. Krankenkor looked up from the submachine gun. "Ah. Herr Haupt, you will have the opportunity to meet with the captain of the Bitburg Group who will lead the assault on the Documentation Center."

The neo-Nazi *Sturmbannführer* went to the front door and returned with a tall blond man in his early twenties.

"Uwe Hartman." Krankenkor introduced him.

The handsome young man glanced at Von Blutliebe and Haupt casually, almost arrogantly, as he stepped into the room. He dug his hand into his pocket and pulled out his own blood-red arm band with its black swastika centered in the white circle. He slipped it over his wrist and up his sleeve.

"Gentlemen," said Krankenkor, "Uwe is also the star of one of Berlin's finest soccer teams. But his other talents are not so well-known publicly."

Uwe smiled and sauntered over to an armchair that faced the three men on the other side of the room. He threw himself into it, sitting casually with one leg up over the arm, and observed then, "The bomb at the train station in Hannover last week, for example. I found two Jewesses from America who had missed the train to Paris and ended up in Germany by mistake. I asked them to hold my bag, which contained the bomb, while I got information for them. I timed it to within less than a minute." He laughed. "It was amusing."

"Uwe," von Blutliebe addressed the youth kindly, like an indulgent father. "Herr Haupt is formerly of the CIA. Now he works...privately. You will work with him in Berlin."

Uwe raised his right arm with the elbow bent and hand flat in a casual salute. *"Sieg heil,"* he said.

Von Blutliebe lifted the MP40 from Krankenkor's hands and tossed it across the room at the blond soccer player. Uwe caught it with both hands, his eyes wide with delight.

"That is the weapon with which we conquered Europe," von Blutliebe told him.

Uwe held it reverently, like a boy presented with a long-desired Christmas toy. He grasped it tightly, opened the folded metal stock and shoved it against his midriff. He aimed it at the three men across the room and imitated the sound of automatic fire.

"Ah-ah-ah-ah-ah-ah-ah," he cried, weaving the barrel of the gun back and forth as if he was mowing them down. They watched him. Uwe smiled and shook his blond hair out of his eyes. "I like it," he said, smiling. His bright blue eyes shone with joy. "With these we shall liberate the gold. And kill whoever stands in our way!"

7

"Talking the U.S. Embassy into getting you out of here was like chewing lemons," Walker Jessup commented as he, O'Toole and Barrabas walked out the prison under the reproachful eyes of the matron. The Fixer's rented Peugeot took them quickly into the city to a suite of rooms at the Hotel Krasinsky on the Dam Square, across from the Royal Palace.

Jessup immediately got on the phone, cajoling State Department friends for military passes for the two men in Berlin. The eastern side of the city was the capital of the Communist German Democratic Republic. But it was also the Russian sector of what was still an occupied city. The British, French and American forces who controlled the western side had occupation privileges to travel at will in the eastern sector. Freedom of movement would be needed by the two mercenaries.

After a shower and a change of clothes, Barrabas sat down to examine the briefing papers on the American spy named Tom Brown, which Jessup had given to him.

The agent came from one of America's wealthiest families. He grew up in big houses, went on nice vacations and was educated at the most expensive schools. Ostensibly he traveled the world as a businessman, and his career profile showed an astonishing variety of entrepreneurial endeavors in various countries around the world.

In actual fact, Brown and the CIA had been using his business pursuits as a sophisticated cover for secret-service activities.

In this career, Tom Brown had a solid-gold performance record, consistently providing the White House with some of its most valued intelligence information.

So what went wrong?

The file contained psychological profiles, including a memo from a doctor who used many words, many syllables, to say he didn't know.

It was an exaggeration to say that Barrabas and Brown were friends. Barrabas had met Brown when he was an intelligence officer in Washington and Saigon. He worked the embassy cocktail circuit to gather military intelligence. Brown was always there, the American businessman who was the life of the party. He was witty, urbane and famous for the amount of vodka he could put away with no visible effect.

Neither man had ever admitted to the other what his real business was. Barrabas had always suspected that Brown was CIA, and Brown certainly must have known that Barrabas was from MAC. They became drinking buddies after going off together after some high-powered affair to clear their heads of people who dangled cocktails like nooses.

Eventually something came between them.

Barrabas spent months coaxing a Hungarian diplomat to give him information on a suspected ARVN invasion, and finally the man was about to come through. He reported back to MAC, which routinely forwards information to the CIA. But the CIA doesn't necessarily reciprocate. Someone had got to the Hungarian before Barrabas.

Finally, somewhere in Saigon, he spotted the Hungarian with Tom Brown. He let them see him. After that, the Hungarian diplomat avoided Barrabas completely.

The last occasion that Barrabas and Brown went drinking together, Brown had looked him in the eye and held up a glass of vodka. "To competition," he said.

Barrabas never saw him again. The transfer Barrabas had requested out of MAC and back to frontline duty came through.

Now that he knew Tom Brown's background, it became apparent that the spy had also been hustling the Hungarian diplomat for information and getting it to the CIA before Barrabas got it to MAC. But why would he woo the guy away from Barrabas?

There was one, obvious answer. For the same reason he wouldn't come in from the cold right now—Brown must be a double agent. Barrabas's job seemed straightforward enough. Either bring the spy back, or find out why he's not coming. That was the way Jessup had put it.

But the last page of the briefing papers put it differently, "Routine procedures will be taken to terminate the threat, should he prove to be disloyal."

That didn't mean Barrabas had to pull the trigger. The CIA had enough agents in enough places who were only too glad to do it.

There was one other detail he remembered about Tom Brown that the briefing papers failed to mention. Brown hated guns, never carried one, but he could do some cute tricks with a knife.

Not that it mattered. If Tom Brown wouldn't come back of his own accord, his life and the skills he had developed to protect it weren't worth shit.

Liam O'Toole came into the room and fell into the chair beside Barrabas, just as the mercenary leader threw the briefing papers aside.

"What are we doing for firepower, Colonel?"

Barrabas glanced at his watch. It was after five. The light outside was fading as the sun fell in the west.

"Paying a visit to an old friend of mine," the leader said, standing.

Barrabas and O'Toole flagged a taxi in front of the hotel, and a little while later they climbed out by a canal in the Jordaan, an old working-class neighborhood of Amsterdam. The cobblestone street was deserted. Barrabas led O'Toole down some stone steps to a concrete embankment at water level. A small wooden rowboat was tied to it, bobbing gently on the water of the murky canal. Barrabas climbed in it and sat on the middle seat facing the stern.

"Come on," he told O'Toole, untying the ropes. The former sargeant looked confused.

"Whose is this?" he asked.

"This is first-class service to the craziest place to buy guns I've seen yet."

O'Toole climbed aboard, rocking the boat and sitting heavily. Water travel was O'Toole's least favorite method.

Barrabas pushed the boat away and dipped the oars into the water. With long powerful strokes he quickly propelled the boat forward almost half a mile down the canal. They passed under a low bridge and turned into a second canal. A little farther they came to a small inlet surrounded on three sides by high old buildings and warehouses, their windows and doors shuttered and bolted against the night. The only light came from the lamps farther down the main canal. Barrabas lifted the oars inside the boat as it washed against a door set at water level in the rear of a five-story building. He tied the boat to an iron ring set in the stone wall and carefully stood, holding on to the door handle for support. He turned the handle and the door opened into complete darkness. Barrabas stepped inside.

"Come on," he called softly to O'Toole. Barrabas's eyes shone in the pitch-black doorway. O'Toole made his way slowly along the tiny swaying rowboat to the doorway. Barrabas reached out, gripped his forearm and pulled him up into the darkness.

They stood on a stone floor. Somewhere rats were scuffling, disturbed by the arrival of the uninvited strangers. The air smelled odd, like a mixture of machine oil and straw.

"You lead, Colonel," O'Toole said skeptically.

Barrabas moved ahead as though he could see in the blackness. O'Toole followed closely. Twenty feet later they stopped. O'Toole heard the sound of a metal latch. A door swung outward and with it came an arc of yellow light from an inner room. Barrabas walked through with O'Toole behind him and closed the door.

They were on the ground floor of a warehouse, filled with barrels of what looked like onions. The air was dusty and sweet with the scent of organic material.

"Tulips," Barrabas said out loud, seeing the Irishman looking around. "But that's not Joey's main line of work. Joey!" he called loudly. There was no answer. He called again.

O'Toole picked a handful of small, flaky bulbs from a barrel. "Well, if he's not here, maybe we can just help ourselves to a supply of these. To go with the white picket fence."

Barrabas looked at him, not understanding the reference.

Both men heard metal clicking together. For two veteran fighters, the sound of a gun being cocked was unmistakable.

Suddenly a dark steel snout protruded from the wooden barrel in front of O'Toole. Tulip bulbs erupted in all directions, spilling over the sides and tumbling onto the floor. A head appeared, followed by two small hands clasped firmly to the butt of an enormous Magnum.

The muzzle roared just as Barrabas turned to see it. It roared again, belching smoke. The bullets' trajectory took them past O'Toole at eye level. There was noise from behind them. A dark-coated figure was jumping out from behind a stack of boxes and barrels. Bloody blisters bubbled across his middle, spraying their load as the bullets pounded out fist-size holes in his chest.

The body fell, coming straight down on Barrabas. He raised his arm and pushed it sideways, where it landed headfirst in a barrel. The body dangled, a knot of arms and legs.

O'Toole stared wide-eyed at the little man standing up to his chin in the barrel of tulips. The snout of the Magnum traveled back and forth from one man to the other as he decided whether or not to shoot.

"Barrabas, you are one lucky son of a bitch," the little man said. He was an American. He shook his head grimly, lowered the gun and started to climb out of the barrel.

Barrabas stood with his hands on his hips, towering like a giant over the tiny, fierce man and chuckling.

"You told me only your friends came in the back way, Joey," the big man said. "So, why are you in a barrel waiting for your buddy to come out of hiding?"

The little man with the gun scrambled over the edge of the barrel finally and stood on his feet. Liam O'Toole couldn't help it. He stared, with a look of amusement on his face. Standing erect, Joey barely came up to the Irishman's waist.

Joey saw the look on O'Toole's face and bristled, his dark, wiry eyebrows arching together and threatening, "That's right fella! I'm a dwarf in case you hadn't noticed. One of the Little People." He swung the Magnum around in a circle and brought it to rest, aimed between O'Toole's eyes. "Got that?"

Barrabas laughed again. "Joey, this is my partner, Liam O'Toole. Someone I've known since Nam."

Joey looked at O'Toole doubtfully. The merc extended his hand and slipped into the Irish brogue of his native land. "'Tis always a privilege and a joy to meet one of the Little People. 'Tis a sign of good luck." Joey looked at the hand a few seconds as his reluctance faded. He shook it.

"Any friend of the colonel's is a friend of mine. Are you the one who sprung this guy from jail?"

O'Toole and the Colonel looked at each other. "Well, I guess you could say something like that," O'Toole answered slowly.

"I knew it was you," Joey told Barrabas. "The papers said a tall white-haired man, so I had the feeling. What in hell were you doing up there on the dikes? Looking for trouble?"

Barrabas looked sheepish. "Forget it, Joey. It's done with now. You tell me what you were doing in this barrel, covered with tulip bulbs. And your friend—who's he?"

"Another Libyan," Joey said simply, shaking the body in the barrel. There was obviously no life in it. He wiped his hand. "Khaddafi is pissed with me. He thinks I sent him a shipment of rusty rifles and screwed them. Me!—" the dwarf's voice rose in indignation and he put his hand on his chest "—Joey Tahone, the fairest, squarest arms dealer north of the Mediterranean! Would I do that to the Libyans?" Seeing the body again, he roared angrily. "The Libyans are jerks! They send these after me like cockroaches, which I step on and squish and exterminate in a variety of ways!" The dwarf kicked the barrel in his rage as hard as he could, sending a look of pain streaking across his face as his foot bounced off the wooden barrel. For a moment he hopped. "What are you looking for Barrabas?" he roared even louder.

"Just guns. Personal weapons for Liam and myself. Automatics. Maybe a submachine gun."

"And some explosives." O'Toole added. "Plastics always come in handy."

"Anything is possible," the dwarf said. "And I got a clearance sale on infantry-support vehicles for immediate delivery! Follow!" He waved his little arm at them and waddled quickly toward a freight elevator at the back of the warehouse. "Secondhand, but only slightly used in domestic riots. I can give you a great deal."

They crowded into a tiny elevator, which took them slowly up five stories. At each floor, Joey stopped the elevator with a key and flicked the lights on briefly. On the first floor he announced "Miscellaneous gear, fatigues, tents, C-rations and jeeps." The room was piled high with enough material to outfit a standing army.

At the second floor he stopped the elevator briefly again. "Combat aids—intruder alarms, mine detectors, optical devices, radar." A similar spectacle presented itself on the third floor—mortars, grenades, launchers, mines and at the far back wall O'Toole spotted a selection of missiles, including the deadly French Exocet.

"They're duds," Joey said, seeing what caught the merc's eye. "I can supply Exocets, Harpon, Milan, Cobra, Tow and the M47 Dragon," Joey rhymed off some of the most popular NATO brands. "But I need two weeks' notice. On hand I do have some Stinger anti-aircraft guided..."

"Just personal small arms," Barrabas reiterated. "We're going light."

"You can get *anything* in Amsterdam," O'Toole muttered.

Joey turned the key and the elevator resumed its climb, past the darkened fourth floor—"Support vehicles, but you already told me you're not intersted," Joey said almost sadly. "Too bad. I got some new stock coming in and I need the floor space."

Finally they arrived at the fifth floor, and Joey opened the slat doors of the elevator. He used his key in a switch to turn on the lights.

The walls on each side of the two mercs were covered with an array of automatic rifles and pistols, submachine guns and machine guns of various Eastern and ComBloc manufacture.

Joey strutted from the elevator and went behind a long counter. He flicked some more light switches, and a series of low spots at the far end of the long room illuminated a row of man-shaped targets. Fluorescent circles marked the kill zones on their chests. The top floor of the old Dutch warehouse was an indoor rifle range.

Joey, whose head was barely visible over the top of the counter, dealt out automatic weapons like cards on the wooden surface. He disappeared under the counter and came back up with an armful of submachine guns.

While Joey laid them out, Barrabas glanced at them with a practiced eye, searching for favorites. He picked up a Browning HP. With a 13-round mag, high velocity and long range, it was a good, reliable weapon.

He put it down and selected an Uzi. A submachine gun would be a good choice for a job like this one that involved an urban environment. Especially since the Uzi came with a 40-round mag. It was small, light and dependably deadly. Unfortunately it was a little too long to be easily hidden—especially with the mag inserted. Nearby was a Beretta 93-R, also an excellent gun. The Beretta was easily hidden on the body, but it had a hell of a kick. The recoil made it hard to control the line of fire on anything but short bursts.

He spotted a Walther MPK and a Heckler & Koch MP5, and was about to examine them when Joey's head popped up behind the counter again. He slapped an unfamiliar submachine gun into Barrabas's hand.

"Give this a go. It's new. Just in from Finland. It's a Jati."

"Looks more like a machine pistol than an SMG," Barrabas commented, wrapping his hand around the grip. The hard plastic grip was mounted on the blue metal gun in a higher position than normal and incorporated the trigger mechanism and the magazine well.

"I've heard good things about that gun," O'Toole said, looking over Barrabas's shoulder.

The colonel bounced it in his hand to feel the weight. It was barely more than a foot long and weighed about three or four pounds.

"How well does it fire?"

As if in answer to the question, Joey dropped two 40-round double-column straight-box mags of 9 mm bullets onto the counter. "Six hundred rounds a minute travel at 1250 feet per second. Stopping power." He took the gun from Barrabas and folded the handle at the front down. In a minute the gun was stripped and lying in parts on the counter.

"Not even fifty pieces and only five of them are used to fire the bullets," Joey continued. "The barrel can be replaced in about five seconds." He pushed the stripped submachine gun toward Barrabas. "Now you tell me what's different."

The colonel picked up the frame and examined it. It only took him a few seconds to say, "The bolt isn't straight. It's angled upward."

Joey took the gun away again with a big smile. "On recoil it travels back at an angle of almost seven degrees," he explained. "That pushes the gun down. Now with the handle mounted as high as the bore line, it gives the shooter leverage. No recoil—total accuracy!" As he talked he reassembled the gun almost as quickly as he had taken it apart. "Try it." He shoved a 40-round mag in and pushed it across the counter.

Barrabas took it and walked to the red line painted along the floor, seventy-five feet from the man-size targets at the other end. Joey pushed a switch that gave full illumination to one of the targets. Barrabas pulled the front handle down and tucked the SMG into his side.

"With one hand!" Joey called to him.

Barrabas turned around and looked at the dwarf doubtfully.

"Go ahead!" Joey urged him. O'Toole shook his head, refusing to believe the gun was as good as Joey made it out to be.

"Where the selector?" Barrabas asked, looking the gun over again.

"There isn't one. For full auto, just press harder on the trigger."

The big man nodded and held the small Jati in front of him, his arm extended and straight at the elbow. He aimed down the sights and pulled the trigger.

The small lightweight automatic pistol chewed bullets from the mag and spat them, ejecting a steady even stream of spent brass casings from the side. As he shot off the entire forty rounds on full auto, his arm floated in front of him. There was definitely a recoil, but it was so mild he could barely see it. If anything, it seemed to make his arm steadier. His grip on the gun never loosened.

A few seconds later the mag was emptied, and the floor covered with the spent cartridges.

Joey fiddled with the lights again, dimming those that illuminated the targets and turning on others behind the cutouts, so the light shone through the newly made bullet holes.

Barrabas whistled. Out of forty rounds, thirty-six were in the target. Joey appeared at his side with a fresh mag and took the gun. The little man held his arm out and aimed at a second target. He fired the entire mag off single-handed.

"With a little practice," he said. The Jati had put all forty rounds in the target, most of them in a five-inch spread around the chest area.

The two mercs and the arms dealer spent another half hour firing off rounds from varying distances at the targets in Joey's shooting gallery. They practised stripping and reassembling the fifteen-inch-long SMG, and using it from the shoulder holster, which could be concealed completely under a light jacket. It was an excellent security weapon.

"Two?" the dwarf asked for their order. "With shoulder holsters or detachable stocks?"

"Give us four of them," Barrabas said, "with stocks and holsters and about two thousand rounds. If you can guarantee they won't bust on us in the middle of something dangerous."

"I guarantee," said Joey enthusiastically. "A lifetime warranty. If it gives you trouble, you bring it back to me."

Barrabas laughed. "Joey, in our line of business, if it gives us trouble, we won't be around to complain."

"So you have troubles," Joey said rolling his eyes. "I promise you, this gun will be a good friend. I sell it only to my favored customers. The Libyans—they got rusty M-16s. But you, Barrabas, only the best."

The Colonel and O'Toole also picked out a couple of HPs with silencers for backup weapons, and O'Toole took a pouch containing ten ounces of plastics with some cord for detonation. It was enough for minor surgery on locked doors or barred windows.

When they went back downstairs, Joey packed the weapons in leather cases. "Nine thousand dollars," the dwarf said as he finished.

"Put it on my bill," Barrabas said, taking one of the cases.

"Barrabas," Joey said wearily. "We have a policy." He tapped on a sign on the wall behind him. Under the Stars and Stripes it read, In God We Trust. All Others Pay Cash.

"Especially in your line of work," Joey added. "Giving you credit is like giving you a warranty, except for one terrible difference."

"What's that, Joey?"

"I lose instead of you."

"So let's make a deal, Joey. If this gun is as good as you say it is, I'll be back with the money. On my word. Deal?"

Reluctantly, the little man nodded. "Deal." He reached up to shake hands with the tall colonel. "You are the only man in the world I trust like this."

On the way out, the dwarf took his own silenced Magnum from his belt. Barrabas and O'Toole followed him to the door they had entered an hour earlier.

Outside, the rowboat floated lazily on the dark waters on the canal. The dwarf put his hand up to stop the two mercs from passing. He put his finger to his lips, urging them to be silent. Then he listened.

Slowly he leaned forward out the door and fired the silenced Magnum upward at the facade of the warehouse. Small flashes of orange sparked from the barrel as it coughed delicately.

The men heard a short mangled scream, quickly stifled. A body dropped from somewhere above the door and splashed into the canal. It bobbed to the surface, rolled over and floated facedown.

"Damn Libyans," Joey cursed, stepping aside to let the mercs pass. He shook the smoking Magnum at the two soldiers. "Nine thousand dollars, Barrabas. Or your name's mud."

8

That evening, at a playing field in a suburb of West Berlin, banks of halogen lights on forty-foot-high steel posts poured artificial daylight onto a soccer field. The digital numbers on the big scoreboard counted the seconds to the end of the game. The home team unleashed a final onslaught on the visiting team's goal. Number 43 passed with a hard kick to number 12. The ball sailed high. Number 12 slipped through two colliding players on the opposite team and ran back with his head up and his eyes on the ball. As it approached he ran forward three meters, jumping up and slamming his head into the ball. He knocked it away from an oncoming player from the opposing team. The ball sailed up. Number 12 swerved forward, deking out another attacking soccer player whose forward momentum sent him splaying on the turf. The way to the goalpost was clear. Number 12 went for it. The ball smashed into the ground, bounced, and his foot connected. It sailed in a slow, graceful arc through the goalposts. The digital numbers ticked off the last seconds to zero, and the new score went up just as the siren sounded game over.

The spectators rose to their feet by the thousands, of a single mind cheering wildly for the winning home team. Then they chanted their hero's name, number

12, the star player of the Berlin League who was surely going to become one of Europe's biggest soccer stars.

"Uwe! Uwe! Uwe!"

Uwe's teammates mobbed the tall blond man, slapping him on the back and grabbing handfuls of his hair to show their affection. Once again, their star had won the game for them.

Uwe broke away from the team and jogged to the center of the soccer field. He stood with his head high and raised his arms over his head in a V, with his fists clenched. The chanting from the fans grew to a roar of triumph, "Uwe! Uwe! Uwe!"

The blond soccer player turned slowly in a complete circle, acknowledging their adulation. Slowly, almost imperceptibly, his raised fists opened and he held his hands flat with the fingers together. The roaring cacophony of his name reverberated across the soccer field.

The German stopped, head high, and his eyes swept across the cheering spectators arrayed in the stands. He dropped his left arm, but for a few moments longer held his right arm straight, hand open, on a slight angle out from his body. It happened so quickly it was almost unnoticeable. Almost, but not quite. The chanting of his name broke into a whistle, cheers and shouts as the soccer fans went wild.

Uwe could feel their energy coming to him, filling his body, giving him strength of iron. He could feel his power. "Sieg heil," he said to himself softly. His arms dropped. He breathed deeply and easily, and jogged off the field to the locker room.

Uwe stripped and walked through the clouds of steam billowing from the shower rooms. His teammates scrubbed down amid good-natured jesting and towel flicking.

"Hey, Uwe," one of them shouted, "a little brain damage never hurt, yes?" He banged his hand on his forehead, referring to the soccer star's last play.

"*Nein*, he has already had a lobotomy. Now he has rocks in there," another shouted over the noise of the showers.

Uwe laughed at them as he adjusted the controls until the water was icy cold. Clouds of steam evaporated from the hot showers around him. Naked men shrieked and scattered from the cold spray.

"This head can do many things," Uwe shouted over the razzing. "I just think where I want the ball to go and presto—it goes!"

"Nay, it's the great god Thor that helps you out, isn't that so, Uwe?" One of his teammates grabbed the blonde's forearm and pointed to a runic sign tattooed on it. Uwe jerked his arm away a little angrily.

"Hey, come on!" his teammate said. "It's not serious."

"Ja," Uwe nodded gravely. "It's very serious."

"All right." The man shrugged, backing off.

Uwe looked across the shower room to his teammate and friend, Wolfgang, who had been watching. Their eyes met.

"We go out tonight, Uwe?" Wolf shouted.

"Ja. Natürlich." Uwe nodded. "Who wants to come with us?"

The question was answered by a chorus of "Where?"

A few other soccer players looked over to their leader and nodded.

"Just to have some fun," Uwe shouted back. "We deserve some fun tonight, don't we men? We are the city's heroes. We can do anything we want." He turned his shower off and grabbed his towel on the way back to the lockers.

A FEW HOURS LATER, Wolfgang turned the wheel of his father's BMW sedan, steering off the main street onto a road that led into the Tiergarten, West Berlin's central park.

"It's not much farther," Uwe said from thc seat beside him. "We'll park just below the monument."

"Hey, Uwe, where are we going?" a mildly drunken voice asked from the back seat. Uwe looked back at his three teammates. A few rounds of heavy beer followed by schnapps to toast the victory had put them in a good mood. It was Gunther who had asked. It was his first time. The others—Wolf, Dietmar and Axel—already knew the score.

"To the Kaiser Wilhelm Memorial," Uwe explained. "We have some work to do there."

"We?"

"It is a club we belong to, Gunther. The Bitburg Patriotic Group. If you perform well tonight, you can join, too."

"What will we do?"

"Dietmar, Axel—" Uwe turned to the two other young men in the back seat "—tell Gunther."

Dietmar began. "There are certain unruly elements, degenerates who come here at night to this park, which is dedicated to the last great German *Kaiser,* to the unification of the German people and to our victories against the French. These degenerates debase it with their activities. The authorities do nothing. . . ."

"But the Bitburg Patriotic Group sees to it that these offences to the dignity of the German people do not go unpunished," Uwe finished. "Park there." He pointed to a space around a closed-down candy kiosk. Wolfgang pulled the BMW over.

The young soccer players piled out. The air was warm from the hot summer day, but here in the park the trees and grass exuded a damp chill that made Uwe shiver. Or was it excitement at what was coming? He couldn't tell.

Wolfgang walked around the car and opened the trunk. He grabbed a pile of hard wooden billy sticks and passed them to Dietmar, Axel and Gunther. Uwe grasped the end of his club tightly and tossed it in the air. It felt good.

High above them on a hillside rising up from the trees, the monument to the *Kaiser* jutted out in a dark outline against the night. The twenty-foot-high bronze statue of the dead king was sheltered by a stone canopy supported by classical pillars. Uwe led off, taking them up the hillside along a narrow dirt path that wound through the underbrush. As they approached the top of the hill, Uwe turned and whispered. "We must now be very quiet." He proceeded again, much slower, and the line of young men silently approached the crest of the hill on one side of the ornate memorial.

Uwe put his hand up to stop them. He saw in the darkness the shapes of two people leaning against the stone base of a pillar. Their white skin reflected light, and the sounds that came from them clearly revealed they were making love.

Uwe motioned with his head to Dietmar, Axel and Wolfgang. The three young men fanned out around the monument. Uwe grabbed Gunther and held him close. Gunther looked up at his hero, the star soccer player.

"The first one is yours," Uwe said loudly.

His words rang out in the night. The young couple stopped abruptly, suddenly aware that they had been discovered. The man turned away, revealing behind him the frightened face of the young woman. He reached down and tried to pull up his pants as she tugged her blouse together. Panic and fear were written across her face. The man was furious.

"Who the hell is out there? Leave us alone! You have no business here!"

"We have plenty of business!" Uwe strode forward, casually but with determination, smacking the billy stick coldly and firmly into the palm of one hand.

The other soccer players moved out from the darkness. The man's eyes flicked across the faces of the young men. He saw their weapons. His face changed. Defiance was replaced by fear.

"Leave us alone," he said. But conviction had left his voice. He hooked his pants together and moved in front of the woman to protect her. She started to cry. "What do you want," the man demanded.

Uwe heard the excited breathing of his companions as they closed in a tight semicircle around the degenerate lovers.

"We want you to learn a lesson," Uwe said. "Gunther!" He jerked his head at the novice who stood behind him. "You first!"

Gunther looked at his leader and swallowed. He felt the eyes of his teammates on him, who were waiting for him to obey. He raised his club threateningly and walked closer to the luckless victims.

"For the Bitburg Patriotic Group!" Uwe shouted. "For the fatherland!"

"Hit him, Gunther!" Axel repeated with bloodlust.

Gunther went closer, his arm raised high and trembling slightly. His face turned ugly as his fist gripped the handle of the club. Adrenaline shot through his system.

"Get the fuck out of here, assholes. Leave us alone!" the desperate man shouted. He was angry again.

Gunther swung.

The man reached out and grabbed the club as it came toward his head. It smacked into his hand. He held it firmly and started twisting as Gunther tried to pull it away. Uwe's lips curled in hatred. He clenched his teeth and emitted an animal snarl. He whipped his club down hard on the man's hand. It cracked against bone and Gunther's wooden club. The man screamed and let go, grabbing his broken hand and holding it. Gunther pulled his club away.

"Again!" Uwe ordered the newest member of the Bitburg Group.

Gunther learned quickly. The soccer player feigned a blow to the man's head. The woman screamed as the man raised his arms to shield himself. Then Gunther drove the club hard into his stomach.

The man belched air. He dropped to his knees with a retching moan of agony. He lost the contents of his stomach.

"Schwein!" Uwe cursed him. He kicked him in the face. The man fell back at the feet of the woman he

was protecting. She was frozen in terror. She looked from face to face of the men encircling her, searching for some sign of mercy.

"Bitte, bitte," she murmured, pleading with them to spare her. "Please leave us alone." But there was no mercy in the eyes of these men.

Uwe raised his club. He swung down with a vicious backhand across her face. Hard wood crunched bone and broke through skull. Blood spurted and her lips gurgled a last helpless noise that grew to a scream for a second or two, then died. She fell back, the side of her face dark with blood.

"Finish them," Uwe ordered, walking out of the circle.

The others closed in, the roar of the approving crowd still rushing through them from the game a few hours earlier. Their clubs rose and fell and rose again until blood dripped down the handles and their hands were sticky with it. Uwe watched his companions beat the degenerates into shapeless blobs of bloody bone.

He grabbed some leaves and wiped the gore from his own club, breathing deeply. The sharp verdant air of the fatherland was invigorating. He watched the others. He had a bigger prize for them now—these were his storm troopers, and with them he would seize the secret of the hidden Nazi gold from the unwitting American army of occupation.

He brushed his blond hair back from his forehead and waited for his pack to finish the slaughter.

9

West Berlin is a walled island floating in the sea of Communist East Germany. Most of the twelve-foot-high, twenty-eight-and-a-half-mile-long concrete barricade ran through parks and lakes in the south, west and northern borders. In the east it went straight through the middle of what had once been the downtown area of the capital city.

Since the end of the war, two new downtowns had been built. In the West there were the brightly lit streets around the ruined memorial tower of a bomb-damaged church at Breitscheidplatz. In the Communist East, garish new hotels circled the tall TV tower and old city hall at Alexanderplatz.

As their plane flew over the city the next morning, Barrabas saw the sunlight glinting on observation decks of the TV tower and the green line that marked the infamous wall down the center of the urban sprawl.

The city was actually separated by two walls, which were about the width of a football field apart. On the long ribbon of grass and mud in between, guard towers appeared at even intervals. No one had to tell Barrabas what else was there—guard dogs, electronic firing devices, land mines and steel antivehicle barricades.

A young marine corporal met the two mercs at Flugelhof Airport and ushered them outside to a waiting car that bore military plates.

"Red-carpet stuff," O'Toole remarked. "Not the usual lot of the mercenary."

"This isn't the usual kind of job," the colonel said. "I haven't worked in a city since I was in Saigon. Urban warfare isn't a preference of mine. It's hard to move, and the advantage always goes to the enemy who lives there and knows the territory."

"Tom Brown?"

Barrabas shrugged. "Who knows. Nothing ever turns out the way it's planned. We're supposed to go over and bring him back. Sounds easy. But it depends on what Brown has in mind."

The young corporal started to put their small, heavy bags into the trunk when Barrabas stopped him.

"Uh-uh. In the back seat. We want them close."

"Why sure," the marine smiled, walking around the car and opening the rear door.

"From Carolina?" Barrabas asked, hearing the accent. He opened the front door and climbed in. O'Toole got in back.

"That's right, sir." The marine sat behind the wheel. He jerked his head toward the back where the valises sat on the seat. "You got guns in there? Sure were heavy enough." He started the car and pulled into the traffic leading away from the airport.

"We were told we would be taken to East Berlin," Barrabas said. "How do we get there?"

"Easy. I drive you. But I'll take you to your hotel here first." The young marine turned up a ramp onto a freeway. A line of trees marked a huge central park called the Tiergarten that led to the Reichstag building and the Brandenburg Gate. On the other side lay East Berlin. From the elevated freeway, the two halves of the city were indistinguishable from each other. Under the high noon sun, the urban landscape sprawled around the greenery of the Tiergarten; long lines of modern buildings had risen from the ruins of the bombed-out city after the war.

"That's East Berlin there," the driver told them, pointing ahead to the tall thirty-story concrete pillar with a silver ball at the top. It was easily the highest structure of the city. "You can always tell the east from the direction of the TV tower."

"We were told the paperwork for us to get through to the other side would be taken care of," said O'Toole, leaning forward from the back seat.

The young marine reached into the breast pocket of his uniform jacket and pulled out a packet thick with documents. "These are your papers," he said. "Colonel Nile Barrabas and Sargeant Liam O'Toole, right?"

The two mercs caught each other's eyes momentarily. Jessup had set it up so their military status was temporarily active.

"Berlin is still an occupied city," the driver continued. "There are four sectors. The French, British and American armies control the West. But the Russian sector is the biggest—almost half the city—and that's East Berlin. Under the occupation agreement, military people can pass freely between the sectors even if ordinary citizens can't."

"Show us the wall up close before you take us to the hotel," Barrabas instructed.

They turned off the freeway and crossed some bridges over a river into a residential and factory area.

Then they turned onto a broad boulevard that led through the Tiergarten. They reached a traffic circle with a high classical column surmounted by a gold statue of a winged angel.

"The Siegessäule," their driver continued his guided tour. "It was built as a memorial to the last war the Germans won, against the French in 1871. The city is full of monuments to wars—except for the last one. But there are still Nazis around. Last night a man and woman were beaten to death right here in the Tiergarten."

"How'd they know it was the Nazis?"

"Swastikas slashed into their victims' skin."

Another half kilometer ahead the famous Brandenburg Gate came into view.

"The wall starts on this side of the gate. South of the park is where the old downtown used to be." As he talked, the driver turned off the boulevard and soon the two mercs were driving along a canal and entering a built-up, modern part of the city. "Some parts of Berlin are still old," the marine said. "But this section was totally bombed out in the war and rebuilt. Wait'll you see what's ahead."

The modern buildings and busy streets quickly gave way to less traffic. Here and there, older buildings still stood between the modern ones and vacant lots. Empty spaces grew more frequent. Then the redevelopment of the war-shattered city ended.

Nineteenth-century buildings with chipped and decaying stone faces stood like lonely sentinels in the midst of parking lots or fields of chipped and broken stone. Straight ahead of them was the wall, splattered with graffiti and crudely painted murals.

The young marine stopped the car by some wooden steps leading up to a lookout platform. Beside it, an old black-and-white photograph, blown up to billboard proportions, showed a bustling city center of streetcar traffic, vintage autos and ornate old buildings.

"Potsdamerplatz," the young marine told the two mercs. They stood on the lookout platform, gazing at a field of grass and mud on the other side of the wall. "Downtown before the war. This is what's left of it. That's the price a country pays for waging Nazi war."

"When I die, I know I'll go to heaven because I already spent my time in hell." O'Toole was reading the graffiti painted on the wall.

"Weird thing to write on the Western side," Barrabas muttered.

"Look over there." The marine pointed to a low hill on the other side, patrolled by East German guards in long blue coats. "That's all that's left of Hitler's bunker. After the war the Russians bulldozed the ruins of the Chancellery into it and buried it."

A few minutes later, Barrabas and O'Toole left their guide waiting in the car while they installed themselves briefly in their modern hotel room in West Berlin's new downtown area. Half an hour later, they were back downstairs in the car.

"Checkpoint Charlie," Barrabas told the young marine, naming the most famous border crossing in the world.

The car coasted through the city and entered Kreuzberg, a poor residential area of old prewar buildings. They turned left onto Friedrichstrasse and the car slowed. Ahead, in front of a little guard hutment, a sign announced in English, Russian and

French that they were now leaving the American sector. Checkpoint Charlie.

The driver waved to the Yankee soldier, who sat sleepily at a desk inside, and kept going.

The wall came to the edge of the street on both sides. Several rows of staggered metal barriers crossed the street. The iron curtain was tangible. They slowed to a stop at the first barrier and the driver rolled down his window. An East German border guard wearing an ill-fitting blue uniform, tightly buttoned despite the heat, sauntered to the window with a stern expression on his face.

Wordlessly, the marine handed him their papers. The guard flipped through them expressionlessly. He waved to another soldier in a glass guard tower overhead. The barrier slowly lifted. The driver edged the car forward, stopping at the next barrier some twenty feet ahead.

"He has to show the papers to his superior," the young corporal told the two mercs. "Then we'll be waved through."

Before it was all over, they passed through four metal barriers, past steel boxes containing infrared cameras to ensure no one was hiding in the trunk, and were scrutinized by a platoon of unsmiling, heavily armed border guards.

"They shoot to kill," the marine said, passing the last of them.

"Do people still escape?" Barrabas asked.

"A few. Last week a couple of men threw a rope from the roof of a house to someone waiting on a roof on the other side. Then they slid over on pulleys. They did it so fast that by the time the guards saw them it was too late. But it doesn't happen too often anymore. Every time someone discovers a way through, they tighten up a little more. If the guards don't shoot you, the automatic firing devices will."

The last metal blockade swung slowly down behind them and the driver coasted to a stop at the next intersection. The scenery here was a stark contrast to what they had just left behind.

Vacant lots still predominated, but instead of broken stone there were grassy spaces between the high old buildings. To the right, the wide street led past row upon row of towering modern apartment buildings.

Toward the downtown core, Barrabas could see the spires and domes of churches and old buildings. Several lacked roofs, and their stone was blackened by the bombings of forty years ago.

"Here you go, Colonel." O'Toole threw the small valise onto the front seat. The Jatis spilled out of the unzipped top. Both men stripped their jackets off and pulled the shoulder holsters on. Then they stuffed the thin parabellum mags into their pockets. The marine corporal watched, wide-eyed but asking no questions.

"Where to?" he asked finally.

"Alexanderplatz," Barrabas said. "What are your instructions?"

"To ferry you around. That's all."

"You can take the rest of the day off. If anyone asks, we'll tell them we used you until this evening. Can we have our papers?"

The corporal's face lit up at the prospect of a free day. He pulled the documents from his uniform pocket again and handed them to the colonel and O'Toole.

It only took a couple of minutes to drive to Alexanderplatz. The two mercs stepped out of the car on the broad plaza in downtown East Berlin. Public buildings, old and new, surrounded Alexanderplatz. In the center, past gardens of rose bushes and fountains of splashing water, the TV tower soared into the sky. At the base, a series of modernistic white roofs zigzagged crazily in a donut around the central column of the tower. On one side, tourists were lined up for the ride to the top.

Across the street, beside a narrow river and across from a stone cathedral, stood the modern glitzy Palast Hotel. Barrabas glanced at his watch. It was already 2:00 P.M.

A young woman greeted the two big Americans at the desk in the lobby. In dark tan slacks and sport shirts, the two men were dressed like other tourists except for the baggy windbreakers they wore to cover the guns. But their size—both standing over six feet—and well-toned bodies made them stand out from the fleshy Western businessmen, Communist bureaucrats and trade delegates who patronized the elegant hotel.

"We're looking for an American. Mr. Tom Brown, from New York," Barrabas told the desk clerk.

"Ah! Herr Brown!" She smiled, knowing the name immediately. "I will ring his room."

She sat at a nearby switchboard and dialed. After a short time, she returned to the desk. "I'm sorry. There is no answer in his suite. Perhaps you would care to leave a message?"

Barrabas looked around the lobby. On one side, double doors led to a restaurant with a café terrace overlooking the river and the cathedral.

"We'll wait there," he told her. He slipped a twenty-dollar American bill from his pocket and, concealing it under his hand, carefully slid it across the counter.

The woman noticed. "Would it be possible for someone to inform me when Mr. Brown returns?"

Her hand slipped over to rest beside Barrabas's. "Certainly."

Barrabas continued to hold the bill down firmly.

"Without telling Mr. Brown. We want to surprise him. We're old friends."

"Of course."

Barrabas removed his hand. The twenty disappeared behind the counter.

The two mercs strolled through the lobby, ignoring the looks their size attracted as they went into the half-filled restaurant. They had crossed the floor to the doors that led outside when Barrabas put his hand up to stop O'Toole.

He nodded to a far table, near the edge of the terrace. A man in an expensive light-colored suit sat at a little table. His head leaned back and his fedora was pulled down over his eyes, resting delicately on the bridge of his nose. A newspaper lay crumpled in his lap. He was asleep. An empty glass sat on the table in front of him. His hand was still wrapped around the stem. A stack of East German paper money was weighed down by a handful of coins. The man was tanned, about thirty-five, and he hadn't shaved in several days.

Tom Brown hadn't changed in the ten years since Vietnam.

10

"Take a seat over there," Barrabas told O'Toole, pointing to a table near the exit. "If he tries to leave, get in his way."

A white-coated waiter approached them.

"May I help you, sir?" he asked in English.

Barrabas gave him a disarming smile and fingered another twenty.

"We're friends of Mr. Brown's," said Barrabas. "Just arrived from America. It's a surprise."

"Ah." The waiter thought for a moment. "Herr Brown is our *Stammgast*—how do you say—a favored customer. He insists not to be disturbed...."

Barrabas slipped the twenty into the waiter's pocket.

"If you're friends, there can be no problem," he hastily added. "Can I bring you something?"

"What's Herr Brown drinking?"

"Martinis, sir. Vodka martinis."

"Bring a shaker of martinis. A glass for me. And some mineral water."

Barrabas approached the agent's table quietly and turned the chair next to him around. He sat on it, back to front.

Occasionally the sleeping spy emitted a quiet even snore. Barrabas noticed some American dollar bills hidden among the East German marks. American bucks talk loud all over the world, and the langauge is universal.

He saw the waiter approaching with a tray of drinks and put his finger to his lips. Obediently, the waiter put the shaker on the table, then the glass and the water. Barrabas filled his glass with the water and set the bottle out of view under the table. He filled Brown's glass with a martini from the shaker. The two drinks looked identical.

Barrabas moved his leg under the table and shoved Brown's foot roughly aside.

The sleeping agent jolted awake halfway through a snore. His hat fell down his forehead and tumbled into his lap. He opened his eyes in shock, looking quickly around. His right hand instinctively moved toward the inside of his suit jacket, telling Barrabas where the weapon was.

Brown gasped at the tall American with the short-clipped white hair. He blinked twice.

"Nile Barrabas! What in hell's name . . . !"

Barrabas lifted his glass, baring his teeth in a big phony smile. "To coincidence, Tom! You're the last person I expected to see on my sightseeing trip here in East Berlin."

Tom Brown looked at him and returned the smile. Big and phony. Alertness had returned to the man's eyes the moment he awakened. He looked Barrabas up and down before reaching for his glass.

"To old friends," Tom Brown said, eyeing the colonel.

"To competition," Barrabas raised his glass.

Brown gulped his drink back. He closed his eyes as the burning liquid shot down his throat and alcohol hit his bloodstream. He arched his back and shook his head with a groan of pleasure. Then he opened his eyes and smiled at the big man. This time it was half-genuine.

Barrabas drank his mineral water and poured Brown another martini.

"Last time we saw each other was, why let me see..."

"Saigon."

"Saigon. That's right!" Brown snapped his fingers in realization and leaned forward. "So why are you here, now, in East Berlin?"

Barrabas's answer was as direct as the question.

"To get you."

Brown looked at Barrabas a moment. Abruptly he relaxed, sitting back in his chair and looking in another direction.

"Oh." He sipped his drink.

Barrabas waited for him to continue. When Brown didn't, he finally spoke. "They ordered you back and you've refused to go."

Brown nodded. "Yeah. Stands to reason. They think I've turned, don't they?"

"Have you?"

Brown laughed and sipped at the martini again. "Uh-uh." He shook his head fervently, then looked suddenly serious. He gazed across the terrace at the trees swaying a little in the breeze. "They're terminating me. Bringing me in from the cold. Know what that means?" He sounded wistful.

"Your work as an active agent is over."

"That's right. It's a desk job in Washington or retirement on some lousy pension. Not that money's a problem, but a desk sure as hell is. Christ, Nile. I just felt like saying no for a change. So they sent you. I wondered who'd come running."

"Brown, you're marked by the Soviets already. If you don't come back—"

"I'm marked by my side, too. I know. Well, I'll come back. I decided. The jig is up, as we used to say when we were kids." He gulped back the rest of the martini and set the glass down. He almost missed the table, but caught the glass before it fell to the floor. Barrabas noticed the agent's hand tremble slightly. "I'll just go upstairs and get my bags."

"I'll go, too."

Brown looked at him and nodded slowly. "Sure." His half grin acknowledged what Barrabas didn't want to say.

The two men stood to go. Barrabas caught Liam O'Toole's eye at the far table. He gave a short, barely perceptible nod of his head toward the restaurant exit while Brown sorted out the money on the table. Finally he just threw down all the East German currency. "Fuck it," he said. "I don't need this worthless shit anymore."

He threw an American hundred on top of the pile. "Money corrupts."

They left the terrace and returned to the lobby of the hotel. O'Toole was nearby, mingling with the strolling tourists in front of a magazine shop.

"How are we traveling?" Barrabas asked Brown.

"Car. It's down in the parking garage. We can take the elevator straight down from my room." Brown turned for the elevator. Barrabas looked in O'Toole's direction. The Irish-American soldier nodded once.

Barrabas followed Brown to the elevator, and the two men rode silently in the crowded car to the fourteenth floor. The summer tourist season was at its height, and the casually dressed hotel guests who rode with them spoke a babel of langauges. Most of them were Eastern European tongues Barrabas couldn't place.

"East Berlin is a popular city for Eastern Bloc tourists," Brown explained quietly. "By our standards it's pretty tame. But behind the iron curtain it's considered sin city. The discos stay open until five in the morning."

Brown's room could have been in a modern hotel in any major American city. The furniture was functional rather than decorative and was bolted to the floor. The wallpaper was some kind of beige fabric. The only thing that gave the location away was the view of Alexanderplatz and the TV tower. A bottle of Polish vodka stood in a bucket of melted ice, a bottle of vermouth beside it.

Brown opened drawers and quickly threw his belongings into an expensive leather suitcase. Barrabas looked out the window, occasionally casting backward glances to check Brown's progress. A brooding silence filled the space between the two men. He heard Brown unscrewing the cap on the vodka and turned around. The spy was pouring it into a silver hip flask and shaking.

"Thirst quencher," he explained, sticking it in his back pocket. He flipped another C-note from his wallet to the dresser.

"You're easy with your money," Barrabas commented.

"I'm easy, period." Brown winked. He threw his key on the bed and picked up his suitcase. Barrabas followed him out of the room.

There was a long wait for the elevator. Two overweight men in polyster leisure suits of strangely iridescent colors chatted and joked in the corridor nearby. It was a language Barrabas didn't recognize.

"Bulgarian," Brown said quietly. "Some agricultural trade delegation."

"Are those suits for real?"

The CIA agent chuckled. "To them they are. The latest in Western fashion. Or their version of it."

A third man emerged from his hotel room and greeted his two comrades as the elevator arrived. It was empty.

They all boarded. Brown pressed the bottom button for the underground parking garage. The three Bulgarians stood in front of them. They bantered and chortled at incomprehensible jokes.

Barrabas looked at Brown. The man was staring off into space, lost in thought. The three Bulgarians didn't press their floor. The elevator slowed at the eighth floor.

The Bulgarians stopped laughing. Two of them turned around, the ugly snouts of their handguns pointed at the Americans' chests.

This wasn't a joke.

The third Bulgarian jammed a key into the elevator control panel and turned it. The doors stayed shut and the elevator continued its descent to the parking garage. One of the Bulgarians, a short stocky man with a broad, flat face and too much nasal hair, spoke first, in heavily accented English.

"Gentlemen, perhaps it is better that you raise your hands."

The Americans hesitated. Brown cast Barrabas a quick look.

"Yes. Immediately." The Bulgarian had his gun cocked.

Brown dropped his valise. They raised their hands halfway.

"Is this one of your colleagues in the CIA, Mr. Brown?" the Bulgarian asked, pointing the snout of his gun at Barrabas. "You, we have been ordered to keep alive. It seems our friends in the Stapo have many questions to ask you about some activities that do not conform to those an American spy is usually engaged in. As for this one—" the Bulgarian waved his gun at the colonel "—we have no instructions. So perhaps it will not matter if we kill him." He broke into a smile and turned to share the joke with the big galoot in purple polyester who stood beside him.

The goofy guy laughed. He thought it was real funny. Barrabas thought it was funny, too. The laugh, not the situation.

"You gotta be the biggest, dumbest creature I ever laid eyes on," he said to the giant.

The big Bulgarian stopped laughing and looked hurt. He grunted a question at his leader.

"Vacos does not speak English, Mr. American," the first Bulgarian said. "He is big and dumb. The perfect killer."

"Yeah, and what about you?" Brown began, picking up where Barrabas had left off. "Anyone who wears a lime-green suit has to be pretty dumb, too."

This time it was the Bulgarian leader's turn to be upset. He stopped smiling.

Brown laughed, throwing his head back and looking at Barrabas. "Can you imagine wearing a suit like that?"

Barrabas laughed, too. "Nope. I wouldn't be caught dead in it. Nowhere."

"Stop it! Stop talking both of you!" The Bulgarian was shouting angrily and waving his gun from man to man when the elevator hit bottom.

The third Bulgarian at the control panel turned his key and the doors slid open.

Barrabas moved first. His right hand karate chopped the leader's wrist. The gun fell, clattering onto the floor. Simultaneously, the colonel's left hand clenched and he knuckled the big dumb guy in the throat.

He heard the sound of the Bulgarian's larynx cracking and the man fell against the wall, trying to suck air past his crushed windpipe. Barrabas's right hand grabbed his wrist, forcing him to point the gun up and away. Still possessed of enormous strength, the giant Bulgarian began to fight back, reaching for Barrabas's throat.

The two men locked in mortal combat.

At the door, the third Bulgarian moved for his gun. The leader went down to grab his from the floor. Tom Brown moved.

He grabbed the Bulgarian's jacket and pushed him violently forward, smashing him into the man at the door.

The third guy lost his balance and stumbled out of the open doors into the parking garage.

Into the big strong hands of Liam O'Toole.

O'Toole didn't ask questions. He didn't even take time to wonder. Business was business and this was all in a day's work. He caught the Bulgarian's head like a basketball with both hands wide and smashed it into the concrete wall.

His fingers dug into the man's head, grabbing handfuls of greasy hair. He pulled the head back. The Bulgarian face was dripping blood, the nose was flattened and a couple of yellowed teeth bounced onto the cement floor.

The man was gurgling through his liquid mouth and the gurgle was building to a scream. O'Toole drove it into the wall again. This time the body collapsed underneath him. He let go of the heavy head and stepped back to the elevator.

Tom Brown and the colonel were just finishing up. Brown's opponent lay facedown and very dead on the floor. Brown held his head down with one foot as he used both hands to pull a tightly wedged, ivory-handled knife from the back of the man's neck.

Barrabas and the Bulgarian brute were still locked in combat, but by now the outcome was obvious.

The colonel arm wrestled until his opponent's gun hand was at face level. He started to bend the hand around. Slowly, inexorably, he twisted the Bulgarian's wrist until the barrel was pointing straight into his face. The Bulgarian strained against the American's strength.

To no avail.

He saw it coming. The big black hole in the barrel of his own gun.

Bam! The Bulgarian's big nose turned inside out and the back half of his brain dripped down the elevator wall. Barrabas closed his eyes and mouth against the shower of blood that rained into his face.

He let go. The body slid to the floor. For a moment the dead Bulgarian balanced on his knees. Then he flopped over, burying his face in the body of the dead man in the lime-green suit.

"They must have wanted me real bad," Brown commented, surveying the carnage.

"Why do you say that?" Barrabas asked, wiping gore off his face with the sleeve of his jacket.

"The Bulgarians are their best killers. They only send the Bulgarians when they're serious."

"Dead serious now, by the looks of it," Liam O'Toole commented.

Brown laughed. "Who's your friend, Nile?"

"Liam O'Toole," Barrabas introduced the Irishman, who was dragging the body outside into the elevator with the other two. Barrabas grabbed the dead man's feet to help out, while Brown stepped gingerly around the corpses to grab his valise.

"Like I said upstairs, I wouldn't be caught dead in that suit," Barrabas said as he and O'Toole swung the body into the elevator.

"Victims of fashion," Brown added. He reached around the elevator door, pressed twelve on the panel and turned the key. He darted out just as the doors closed.

"Next stop heaven. C'mon. My car's over here."

11

The American spy led Barrabas and O'Toole to the turquoise Mustang parked in a far corner among rows of Trabants and a couple of Volkswagens. The top was down.

"My pet," he explained. "I had it shipped over a few years ago. It handles beautifully. No one around here's seen anything like it." Then he pushed his suitcase at Barrabas. "You're not going to get very far looking like that."

The colonel looked down. His jacket and shirt were drenched with blood. Brown pulled the silver flask from his pocket, took a swig and handed it to Barrabas.

"Have a drink. And use some of it to wash the blood off your face and hands. Good for stain and memory removal," he added, walking around to the front of the car. "There are spare clothes in my bag."

Barrabas stripped off his jacket and started to unbuckle the shoulder harness that held his Jati. Brown opened the hood of the car and bent down over the engine block.

"Bomb?" O'Toole asked.

"That's right," Brown's voice was muffled. "Just checking. Nope. Nothing here."

O'Toole slid under the rear end of the car and checked around the gas tank. There was no sign of tampering. "Looks okay," he said, pulling himself out. Brown was waiting for him.

"You know about this kind of stuff?" the CIA agent asked.

O'Toole nodded. "Demolitions expert."

Barrabas splashed a handful of vodka over his face and wiped the last of the blood off.

"Could come in handy," Brown mused, looking at O'Toole. He got into the driver's seat while O'Toole got in the other side and Barrabas rode in back. Brown drove the Mustang out of the garage and onto the street as the colonel pulled on a clean shirt.

Rush hour in East Berlin was never heavy. There weren't enough private cars to fill the wide thoroughfares that ran through the center of the modern city. Brown turned right and headed for the bridge over the little river. With the roof down, Barrabas had to shout over the sound of the wind and the traffic.

"How're we going back? Checkpoint Charlie?"

Brown laughed. "Let's be adventurous!" He pointed to a five-level parking garage in the distance. Next to it stood a four-story building with a high peaked roof. Beyond that was the Wall. "I figure if you went full speed through that parking garage and kept going you could land on the roof of the house and drive downhill over the wall."

"Into what?" Barrabas said doubtfully. He pulled a crumpled windbreaker from Brown's bag. It would serve to conceal his SMG.

"Water. There's a canal on the other side. It's quite a game over here, actually, thinking of ways to escape."

"Well, I'd just as soon take the easy way out, Tom," Barrabas said.

O'Toole agreed.

"They know I got the car, so they'll probably be watching the border roads. But there's another way out that's very safe."

"What?"

The spy pointed to an elevated railroad line that ran behind some buildings parallel to the street. "The train. It takes us on the S-Bahn from Friedrich Bahnhof to West Berlin."

"What happens to the car?"

Brown shook his head, a little sadly. "Given a choice between the Mustang and my life..."

"I understand."

Brown nodded. "It's like the choice between love and freedom."

It was just a joke, but for Nile Barrabas it brought back memories of Amsterdam. Love and freedom. Jessup was right. There was nothing like a little action to take a guy's mind off problems with women.

Bahnhof Friedrichstrasse was a central depot not only for the subway, the U-Bahn and the elevated S-Bahn that led to West Berlin, but also as the starting point for the Warsaw Express, the Moscow Express, the Leningrad Express, the Budapest Express and every other express train that led into Eastern Europe.

Today, everyone was traveling.

There were old ladies arriving from West Berlin with shopping bags full of capitalist goodies for Communist relatives, and tall young soldiers in the stiff conscript uniforms of the East German army or in the dress tans of Red Army soldiers on leave from one of the Russian military bases that ringed the divided city.

Brown elbowed his way through the crowd with Barrabas and O'Toole behind him.

He disappeared into the mob that surrounded the ticket offices. Barrabas kept him in view, watching his gray fedora bob over the heads of the crowd. A few minutes later, Brown returned with their tickets. "The S-Bahn is that way," Barrabas pointed to a big white *S* on a blue sign where an arrow pointed upstairs to an open-air platform.

"Right." Brown handed tickets to Barrabas and O'Toole and hoisted his suitcase. "Let's take the center stairs, though. It won't be as crowded."

They began moving when suddenly the CIA agent came to an abrupt stop. People slammed into him from behind, muttering angrily as they pushed past.

"What's the matter?" Barrabas asked.

"Over there." Brown was looking through the crowd to the foot of the long stairs that led down from the open S-Bahn platform. On each side, two big men stood watch like guard dogs, scanning the faces of the crowd that surged up the steps. Both were bald, their pates glistening, and both had small eyes set like steel nuggets in overly fleshy faces. One was tall and wiry and wore a dark trench coat. The other was shorter, about a yard wide, and wore a cheap suit.

"The Russians," Tom Brown hissed sideways to Barrabas and O'Toole. "They always send bald guys."

"Why the Russians?"

"Second string to the Bulgarians, as killers. Everyone knows that."

"I thought I was bringing you in from the cold," Barrabas told Brown. "Seems to me it's pretty hot over here."

Brown smiled meekly. "So what do you suggest?"

"Remember the Bulgarians?"

Brown nodded. "How can I forget?"

"Same thing. Liam, take the short guy, I'll take Mr. Tall. Tom, we'll meet you at the top of the stairs." He looked steadily at the spy. Brown nodded.

"I'll be there."

"You'd better be."

The two mercs separated, leaving Brown to push through the crowd with his suitcase. He had almost reached the stairs when the Russians saw him. The two goons looked at each other through the mob of travelers and nodded. They moved toward the American agent.

Brown saw them coming. He swallowed and pushed harder at a stocky woman in a kerchief who moved up the stairs with monumental slowness. She turned and growled at him, the stubs of her teeth dripping saliva. Brown jumped back, tipped his hat and tried moving around her. The short, stocky Russian was coming his way. His thick arm reached forward and grabbed Brown's lapels.

Brown tried to pull around him, but he was caught fast.

Suddenly the Russky felt something hard and deadly in the small of his back. It felt like a gun. He turned. A big red-haired man with tanned, freckled skin was smiling wanly at him. The man jerked the Russian's head back and pulled firmly on the killer goon's jacket. He let go of Brown and backed up.

Meanwhile, on the other side of the steps, Nile Barrabas slipped through the crowd, taking the smaller HP from his pants pocket. The Russian, intent on intercepting the fleeing CIA agent, didn't see him coming. Barrabas slammed into him.

"Entschuldigen!" he excused himself in German.

He grabbed the collar of the Russian's open trench coat and jerked it down, pinning his arms with the sleeves. The Russian strained for his gun in the holster under his armpit.

"Nyet!" Barrabas said firmly.

He slipped the HP under the folds of the Russian's trench coat to hide it from passersby and dug the barrel into the man's side.

"Just come quietly," he warned the Russian.

They walked back through the crowd, Barrabas prodding him with the barrel of his handgun.

On the other side of the crowd, O'Toole pulled the Russian agent behind the stairs, where some mops and buckets stood in a dark corner. Tom Brown shoved in after them. O'Toole had the killer against the wall when he reacted.

He raised his thick arms and pushed the merc away. He opened his mouth to bellow for help. Suddenly he froze, arrested in midmovement. His mouth opened, but the scream was silent.

Brown had his dagger buried to its hilt in the goon's kidney. Toxic shock. Instant death. Brown gritted his teeth, gripped the handle and twisted.

The Russian beady blues glazed over. All he saw now was Red heaven. O'Toole strained to hold the man's body upright.

"Drag it over there," Brown said, pointing to a row of telephone booths a few meters away.

The two Americans put their arms around the dead man and walked him to the telephone like he was an old drinking buddy. They pushed the corpse inside.

"I'll see if Nile needs help." Before O'Toole could say anything, Brown disappeared.

On the far side of the stairs, Barrabas walked his captive Russian as far as the washroom door before the man made his move.

He jerked his elbows up to free them from the pulled-down sleeves.

It didn't work.

But the move made Barrabas mad.

He clenched his teeth and jerked the HP up, slamming the Russian under his chin. He pushed him through the swinging door as the cruel clack of breaking teeth and lower jaw sent shock waves of pain through the agent's head. Blood burbled from the corners of his mouth.

The toilet door swung closed behind them.

Barrabas pushed the Russian in front of him with his left arm wrapped around the man's neck in a strangle hold and the barrel of the HP pressed against his temple.

The man was trying to scream but he could barely open his mouth. Barrabas walked him across the washroom and pushed him into a cubicle. He kicked the door shut and shoved the man's head into the toilet bowl. The flush handle was hanging from a chain on the wall. Barrabas pulled.

There was a loud gush as water roared out of the holding tank into the bowl. Inundated by the cold flood, the Russian began to struggle. Barrabas pushed his face into the porcelain and pulled the trigger. Gray and red speckled the white bowl momentarily before gushing water washed the lumps of bone and brain away. Barrabas stood up and shoved the gun back in his pants.

The body slumped against the wall of the cubicle, with the killer's head draining into the toilet. It seemed very appropriate.

Barrabas left the washroom as two young men in East German army fatigues walked in.

Outside, hundreds of travelers still jostled and pushed in a steady stream up the wide staircase to the platform. O'Toole was just coming around to get Barrabas.

"Brown's up there," O'Toole told him, pointing up the steps. Barrabas saw the white-suited CIA agent at the top of the stairs just as he disappeared along the platform.

The two mercs pushed their way through the crowd and took the steps as fast as they could. When they got to the top, Brown was far down the platform, walking quickly, suitcase in hand. He turned and looked back at them. He kept going. There were trains on both sides of the track. One was a commuter train. The other was a long-distance express; the overhanging sign said Dresden. The porters were pulling up the steps onto the cars, and a basso profundo voice announced through the loudspeakers, *"Zurückbleiben!"* Stand back.

Far down the tracks, near the front of the train, Tom Brown jumped into the doorway of a car. The conductor closed the bottom half of the metal door and leaned forward to pull in the top. A shrill whistle blew and the train began to move.

Barrabas ran.

His legs flew along the platform while he searched for an open door. All had been sealed. The train picked up speed. Barrabas ran faster.

He surged ahead, slowly passing each car, even as the train gained velocity, until the two, man and train, matched speeds. The man gritted his teeth and ran faster. He was almost at the last door, where the upper section was still open. He reached out to grab the edge when the conductor appeared. He shook his head at Barrabas and closed the door.

The train pulled ahead.

Barrabas saw the end of the platform in front of him and braked. His chest heaved painfully as the train left the station. O'Toole drew up beside him, gasping.

"Shit," Barrabas muttered between breaths. His big chest pumped up and down. He swallowed. "So the bastard has turned." His throat was raw from sucking back lungfuls of air.

He watched the train disappear across the center of Berlin as his breath slowed.

"We can still get him," he said to O'Toole.

The Irishman looked quizzically at Barrabas.

Barrabas pointed down the tracks. "That train. It's going to Dresden, about three hours from here. But it'll stop before then at the smaller cities. And either Brown will be getting off, or we'll be getting on."

"The car!" O'Toole said, guessing the colonel's plan.

"That's right," Barrabas said. "And if I can hotwire a bulldozer when I'm drunk I sure as hell don't need keys for that Mustang!"

12

Barrabas and O'Toole quickly returned to the street where Tom Brown's car was parked. Barrabas leaped over the door and stuck his head under the dash. The vintage Mustang was so old it hadn't been equipped with antitamper devices. He soon had the appropriate wires pulled from the ignition. He held two of them slightly apart between his thumb and index finger as he squirmed around and sat up in the driver's seat.

"Got it?" O'Toole was sitting in the seat beside him, watching the street.

"Yeah," Barrabas muttered, pressing the clutch in. He squeezed the wires together. The car engine coughed until he gave it some gas. It roared to life. He pulled the gears into neutral and twisted the two wires together. Then he put the car in gear and pulled into the street.

The narrow U-turn left the tires screeching in a scorched semicircle on the road. He turned toward Alexanderplatz, where overhead highway signs pointed out the directions. One road led to Warsaw. The other one went to Dresden.

Less than half an hour later they crossed the outskirts of East Berlin and drove along tree-lined highways through the German countryside. The light traffic of little East German Trabants posed little problem for the agile American car. Shortly after leaving the city they caught sight of the train running on its track parallel to the highway, about half a kilometer away.

O'Toole searched the glove compartment until he found a map of East Germany.

"Posen is up ahead," he called over the roar of the wind and speed. Barrabas was matching the train's speed, but staying a short distance behind it.

"What?" he shouted back.

"A town called Posen, about ten kilometers from here. It's fairly big. Unless it's an express train, it'll stop there."

Barrabas floored it.

They beat the train into the small city by less than a minute. Barrabas left the car and slammed the door behind him. "If I'm still on the train when it leaves the station, head for Leipzig," he told O'Toole. "I'll meet you there."

"With Brown or without?"

Barrabas shrugged. "At this stage, I'd say he'll be with me, dead or alive."

He walked through the small empty station and out the far doors to the platform. A dozen or so passengers from Berlin had just stepped off. Barrabas walked over to the train, scanning the windows for a glimpse of the CIA fugitive. The train looked empty. In one compartment, the curtains were drawn over the windows.

He waited for the rest of the passengers to clamber down from the cars. The conductors and porters stood in a group near the station door exchanging small talk. Barrabas turned and went up the steps.

The train was typically European. A long narrow corridor ran along one side of the car with the passenger compartments opening off it. Going slowly down the corridor, he could look into each compartment through glass windows. Some were empty. In others, one or two passengers sat sleeping or reading newspapers. He felt the train vibrate under his feet and suddenly lurch forward again. The pastoral landscape outside slowly slid by as the train left the station.

Barrabas reached the last compartment. The curtains had been drawn over the glass partition from the inside. He put his hand on the door handle and gently turned. The door swung open.

With the curtains on the outside windows drawn together, the compartment was in semidarkness. Tom Brown half jumped from his seat, his hand reaching inside his jacket.

Barrabas beat him to it. The Jati slid easily from its holster.

Brown smiled and sat down.

Barrabas moved inside and closed the door behind him. The train picked up speed as it hit open country.

"So you did turn," Barrabas stated flatly. The Jati remained steady in his hand. "Go ahead," he said, motioning at Brown's hand, which was halfway inside his jacket. "Let's see what you got."

Brown reached inside and pulled out the SS dagger.

"Is that it?" Barrabas sat in the seat opposite Brown, keeping the SMG trained on him.

"Little souvenir," Brown said. He held it up so Barrabas could see the lightning rune of the SS and the swastika. "But I ain't no Nazi." He looked at the knife. Then he used it to clean his thumbnail.

"A Communist instead?" Barrabas stared at Brown, searching for a reaction. The man remained cool. "Or a traitor? A double agent?"

Brown's smile faded. He moved the point of the dagger onto the next fingernail and cleaned it, too.

"No," he said slowly, as if he was thinking it over. He looked up at Barrabas. The colonel searched Tom Brown's eyes, trying to figure out what was going on inside his head.

Brown continued to clean his nails, slowly and methodically. "No, I'm not turning. But I guess it looks bad, doesn't it?"

"Doesn't look good."

"They called me in because my cover's blown."

"I know."

"Know what that means?"

"We've already been through this, Tom. Back at the hotel restaurant."

"Come on, Nile. You went through a stint at MAC Saigon a few years back. Remember what it was like?"

Barrabas thought a moment before answering, trying to figure out what Brown was getting at. The Saigon job in military intelligence had seemed promising when he took it. But Barrabas hadn't had the patience for it. He was a fighter, not a secret agent.

"Yeah, I remember," he said finally.

"Desk job!" Brown trumpeted, flourishing the SS dagger, in a little circle by his head. "And you know damn well what you did about it, Nile. You got your ass back out there, didn't you? Requested a transfer to front lines, to active duty. Right?"

"That's right, Brown. So what's it got—"

"I'm just saying I'm not a desk-job kind of guy, Nile. That's all."

"So what the hell are you into? It looks to me like you're working for them." Barrabas waved the gun at the curtained window, and the Communist country outside.

Tom Brown nodded. "Yeah, I guess it looks bad." He was silent a moment and appeared to concentrate on the Nazi knife. Abruptly he changed the subject. "Remember that Hungarian diplomat you were hustling for information back in Saigon?" he asked.

Barrabas nodded slowly.

"He was a double. He was feeding us—I say 'us' because he suckered me for a long time, too—false information mixed in with the good stuff. I figure you always knew I threw him off you. I just offered him more money for the same information. It was easy. But he was just one man in a bigger operation for the other side, and we wanted a few of the others before we got to him. I always meant to fill you in on it after the operation was finished. But by then you were back on active duty. As for the Hungarian, well—" Brown toyed with the knife "—he was eventually eliminated. One of my more subtle jobs. I fed some news to the other side that their Hungarian double was doubling for us, not them. It wasn't true, but the evidence I supplied was carefully manufactured. They executed their own man. A big disappointment for the loyal Hungarian, I imagine."

Barrabas looked at Brown, the Jati still aimed at the man's chest. "What are you getting at, Tom?"

The CIA agent shrugged. His eyes clouded. "I dunno, Nile. I guess I just want to be friends with you."

"You're not making it easy."

Brown nodded, as if he agreed. He used the knife blade to push the curtains away from the window and briefly peered out at the passing countryside. Then he let the curtains fall back and looked at Barrabas.

"You believe me?"

"How can I?"

Again Brown nodded. "Yeah."

"You got any more talking to do?"

Brown waited a moment before answering. "Yup."

"I'm running out of time," said Barrabas. He glanced down at the gun in his hand. Brown understood his meaning.

Brown's hand moved so fast it was a blur and the SS dagger skidded with a quiet whistle past Barrabas's temple. It quivered in the wood panel behind his head.

He squeezed the trigger on the Jati.

The bullet tore across the CIA agent's shoulder and pinged into the metal wall of the coach. Barrabas had jerked his aim to the side instead of killing Brown. The spy hadn't even tried to avoid the line of fire.

"What're you trying to do Brown, commit suicide?"

"Look at the knife. At the engraving on the blade," Brown told him.

Barrabas pulled the dagger out of the wood panel. He glanced at the gleaming steel blade. The name engraved on it in a flowing script was "Ulrich Meser, SS."

"It's a long story," Brown started to explain. "Let's just say that the knife started it all off. I found it with a bunch of other junk in the bottom of a trunk, along with some things that proved that SS Captain Ulrich Meser was alive as recently as 1976."

"So."

"He was supposed to be dead in 1945."

"So, what are you getting at?" Barrabas's curiosity was aroused.

"Ulrich Meser was one of five SS soldiers who were entrusted to hide a hundred million dollars' worth of Nazi gold. The gold has never been found, so they did their job well. According to records seized by the allies after the fall of Berlin, all five SS soldiers are dead—and they took their secret with them to the grave."

"But now this one is still alive. What's he doing, living off the proceeds?"

"Uh-uh." Brown grinned broadly. "As far as I know the gold is still hidden. Meser hasn't touched it. And I know where Meser is, right now."

"So, do you mind explaining—"

"That's the whole point!" Brown threw his hands into the air in mock frustration. "I've been tracking him down and on the verge of finding him for months now. Finally, yesterday, I got the information. The same day I got the call back to New York. Christ, the timing couldn't have been worse."

Barrabas looked at Brown for a moment, then put the Jati back inside the shoulder holster. He scratched the back of his head with the blade of the SS dagger.

"He's in Dresden," said Brown.

"I thought they didn't like war criminals in this country."

"They don't. They still execute them here. But this guy's hidden—sort of. He's in a monastery. He's a monk, having taken vows of eternal penitence for his war crimes. And the monastery he's in has traditionally maintained privileges of sanctuary that date back to the middle ages. Even now the Communist government doesn't dare violate the tradition. I guess they figure Ulrich Meser has found his own prison." The spy leaned forward on his seat and spoke in conspiratorial tones.

"Want to come, Nile? See what we can find out?"

Brown threw the colonel a smile that was almost a taunt.

Barrabas remained expressionless. Either Tom Brown had stumbled onto the biggest secret left over from the Second World War, or he was feeding him the biggest crock he'd heard in a long, long time. Either way, he had to hand it to the spy for pushing the right buttons. Barrabas couldn't resist a challenge, even if it was just the opportunity to see what Tom Brown really had up his sleeve. And he knew damned well if he turned it down, he'd regret it.

"I'll talk to my friend..." Barrabas said, starting to smile.

Brown was getting excited. "We'll have a ball!" He reached inside his coat pulled out his silver flask.

Barrabas laughed. "If I know O'Toole, he'll go for it."

Brown stood up and flung the curtains open. "Let's go ask him!" Across half a klik of pasture, the Mustang flew down the East German highway, keeping an even pace with the train.

Barrabas laughed again. "Seems you're always a step ahead, Tom."

"Damn betcha, Nile."

Barrabas's right hand blurred suddenly. The SS dagger chunked into the wall behind Brown's head and shivered from the violent impact.

"Just don't move too fast," Barrabas told the CIA agent. A few drops of red gathered along the rim of Brown's ear where the dagger had skimmed it.

13

At Stapo headquarters in East Berlin, Ilsa shook with anger. She had just read the report that she held in her hands. The three mangled corpses in the elevator at the Palast Hotel had caused quite a frenzy among a group of Rumanian opera singers when the doors opened on the twelfth floor. And the two dead Russians at the train station meant the word would come down from Moscow.

"B-b-but we did send in the Bulgarians," a nervous aide said to her, trembling and avoiding her eyes for fear of incurring deeper wrath.

"Yes, that's right. And the Bulgarians are our best killers." Ilsa paced furiously in the narrow room.

She turned abruptly and faced the aide, gesturing with the report. "But I am good, too," she said earnestly. Her eyes glowed. She held up her left hand and flashed the long, deadly red nails slowly. "In fact, I am better."

With a single backhand stroke so swift it was merely a blur, she slashed the report into six even strips. "The Bulgarians were boobs! Now it's my turn!"

Ilsa sprinkled the shreds of the report slowly and contemptuously onto the floor.

"There is only one place where we will find the American spy now," she said.

"But the monastery is beyond the law!"

"But not beyond Ilsa." The aide gulped.

"And the Americans who called for him at the Palast Hotel?" he asked timidly. "What of them?"

A look of consternation crossed Ilsa's face. "Yes. Whoever these mysterious strangers are, they will likely be with him. Herr Brown I will keep alive until he answers my questions—and perhaps longer, for entertainment. But the other two can die immediately."

"Do you wish for a car right away?" the aide asked, eager to appear less nervous and more helpful.

Ilsa nodded. "We leave for Dresden on the double."

WITH O'TOOLE DRIVING, Barrabas beside him and Brown in the back seat, they approached Dresden on the highway that ran along the Elbe River, coming down into a valley from the rolling hills overlooking the city. On one side of the river were the nineteenth-century neighborhoods of five-story gray apartment buildings. On the other side, linked by bridges, was the old city—what was left of it.

"The fire bombing in the Second World War killed about two hundred thousand people," Brown told Barrabas and O'Toole as the city grew large on the horizon.

"I remember," said Barrabas. "More than died in Hiroshima." It was a story every soldier knew. On one night half the city had been reduced to rubble. The firestorm had been so strong it had sucked all the oxygen from the surrounding area. Those who didn't blow up in the explosions, burn in the flames or bake in the bomb shelters had suffocated. Now they were driving past the modern high rises that had replaced the old city. Near the river, several of the palaces had been restored. The ruins of an old cathedral had been left as a permanent reminder of the destruction of war.

"It used to be one of the most beautiful cities of Europe apparently," Brown mused.

"I suppose you can say it was a tragedy," said Barrabas. "But I can't get too upset about it. The tragedy of Dresden was nothing compared to what Nazi Germany did to the rest of Europe. Warsaw, for example. When the Poles rose up against their overlords, the Nazis reduced the entire city to a field of rubble."

The three men rode in silence for a while. The highway circled the city, crossing the Elbe on the eastern edge. Following Brown's directions, O'Toole drove off the highway onto a secondary road that led through quiet fields and quaint German villages into the rolling hills of Lower Saxony.

"This job is taking a little longer than it was supposed to," Barrabas said to O'Toole.

The Irishman shrugged. "It's not every day I get to go off in pursuit of Nazi gold, Colonel. The rest of the SOBs are going to be jealous as hell."

"Not to mention your wife."

O'Toole thought about that for a minute. Then he nodded. "This is what happens, isn't it?" he said. "With women? Promise them anything. Promise them they're number one. But put a mission in front of us and we're off like bloodhounds with the scent."

"Yeah. It's like an addiction. I thought Erika understood. But I guess she didn't. I don't think anyone can who hasn't had the feeling."

O'Toole nodded. "We have to talk, Colonel. After all this is over."

"You still thinking about pulling out?"

O'Toole nodded. He looked away from the road to catch the colonel's eyes briefly. Barrabas was smiling at him. The colonel slapped his old sargeant from the Vietnam war on the shoulder.

"We'll talk, O'Toole. Whatever you decide, I'll understand."

"You'll like Susy, Colonel," O'Toole said. "She's the best thing that ever happened to me."

"There it is." Brown's voice boomed from the back seat. He pointed to the hillside ahead of them, where an ancient stone wall surrounded an old castle. A gravel drive opened abruptly onto the road. O'Toole swerved hard to the right and braked as the Mustang bounced onto the rough gravel.

The road wound in and out among the trees as it climbed the hillside. Finally O'Toole braked in front of a high stone gate. There was a wooden bridge over a ditch filled with dirty water.

"It's got a bloody moat," O'Toole muttered, staring up at the ancient walls.

"Beware of crocodiles," Brown warned, laughing. He jumped out of the back seat over the side of the convertible, as Barrabas and O'Toole got out. The three men walked slowly over the drawbridge until they stood in the shade of the gateway. Beyond was a sun-filled courtyard surrounded on all sides by stone walls with small slits for windows.

A young man in the brown garments of the monastical order approached and addressed them in German.

Tom Brown answered in the same language.

"Gentlemen, may I help you?"

"We have come to meet with Brother Ulrich," Brown told him. "We're from the American Horticultural Society; Brother Ulrich's work has acquired an immense reputation."

The young monk smiled with delight.

"Horticultural Society?" Barrabas muttered, puzzled.

"I didn't know you understood German," Brown said, smiling at him.

"Special Forces training at Bad Tolz, in Bavaria," Barrabas explained.

"I had no idea his reputation had spread so far," the monk said enthusiastically. "Please come this way, gentlemen. Our monastery is known for its hospitality. And I'm sure Brother Ulrich will be most delighted to see you."

Barrabas turned to O'Toole. "Take care of things out front." The Irishman nodded and waited by the gate as the other two followed the monk across the courtyard toward a stout wooden door on the far side.

"Horticultural Society?" Barrabas said again.

"You'll see," Brown answered mysteriously.

The door opened into a long, dark and cool corridor that led through the building toward bright daylight. They stepped into a large garden, covering several acres, which led from the main buildings to the back walls of the old monastery. Hundreds of varieties of flowers basked in the summer sunlight, their full blooms tossed lightly by a gentle breeze. The air was thick with their smell. The visitors stopped momentarily, taking it in.

"We owe all this to Brother Ulrich's efforts," said the young monk. "His success at breeding new varieties from old species of flowers is a gift of God, surely in reward for his great devotion to prayer and to the welfare of our order."

"Amen," Brown concluded with a secret smirk.

"Not a bad retirement home for a war criminal," Barrabas pointed out.

Brown threw him a warning look. The young monk didn't seem to understand English but it paid to be cautious. Two thirds of the way across the garden another monk poked among the flowers. The hood on his long brown robe was pulled back, revealing him to be an old man with a fringe of stringy white hair around his temples and bushy eyebrows that jutted out from his forehead like a visor.

"That is Brother Ulrich. Come. I will take you to him."

Brown put his hand up to stop the young monk. "Allow us," he said. "We will approach quietly."

Their host looked surprised, but quickly demurred. "If that is what you wish," he said. Silently he vanished back inside the monastery door.

"Let's get this over with," Barrabas told Brown. The CIA man went down the pebbled path that ran between the flower beds. The old monk didn't notice their approach until they were almost on him. He stood up slowly from a bed of roses and turned to them, a gentle smile lighting up his face. He seemed not at all surprised.

"Brother Ulrich?" Brown asked.

The monk nodded. "That is what I am called. May I help you gentlemen?" He looked from man to man, his face an open question. Brown shifted uncomfortably.

"Yes, I think so. Hope so. We need some information."

The monk kept smiling. "You are not Germans."

"Americans."

"Ah. That explains your accent. I have not seen Americans for many years. Now, information?" The old monk turned back to the roses. "Yes, let me explain. This pink rose, for example, is the offspring of that white one and that one over there that is blood red. But alas, the color is not as strong..."

"Not that!" Brown cut him off sharply. His voice softened. "Another kind of information. Captain Ulrich Meser, Waffen SS Totenköpfe Division."

The elderly monk stiffened almost imperceptibly, but remained bent over his precious flowers, gently stroking the petals of one with his thumb. Without turning to look at the Americans, he began to move along the garden, touching the blossoms and pulling them close to sniff their scent.

"How did you find me?" he asked finally, still bent over his flowers, not turning to look at them.

"An old trunk contained your uniform and some notebooks you made in code. They were recent. It was part of a shipment of old furniture out of Dresden."

"Ah." The old man continued to tend his flowers, poking among their stems. "Yes, it went by accident in a load of pieces we sold from the monastery to raise money. My notebooks were a terrible loss. Do you still have them?"

"What are they? A code of some kind—what for?" Brown demanded.

The old monk laughed. "Genetic codes, that's all. For breeding my flowers. Only the purest, the best..." Finally Brother Ulrich straightened and turned to face them. Tears filled the corners of the old man's eyes and fell slowly down his wizened cheeks.

"Do you know how many flowers are in this garden?" he asked them. "Fifty-six thousand, nine hundred seventy-two. One for everyone of my victims. So long ago," he sighed wistfully. "Such a terrible war."

"That's a very accurate count," Barrabas told him.

The monk looked at the tall white-haired American mercenary, meeting his eyes steadily.

"For twenty years I stayed in my cell in the monastery and contemplated. In my contemplation, I counted. I counted the face of every Jew I machine-gunned into pits, every child I drove into swamps to drown, every resistance fighter and hostage burned alive in the barn or church of his own village. I started at the beginning and remembered one by one. How they added up. So many. I remembered the look on every face as each one watched me, their executioner. And when I finished counting, I had counted to fifty-six thousand, nine hundred seventy-two. That is how many times I have seen the eyes of human beings see death. Because that is what I was. Death." The old man paused, looking at the two Americans. "That is how many flowers grow in this garden. Not one more, nor one less. You are the first people who know this. But you are also the first people who have called me by my real name in forty years."

"Your guilt doesn't interest us," Brown said squarely.

"No, I suppose not." Brother Ulrich turned and walked toward the monastery, motioning them to follow with a wave of his hand. "Why have you come? To kill me?"

"No." Brown pulled up in front of him and stopped. The monk waited for him to move out of the way. Brown didn't. "We want to know the location of the gold."

Again the monk laughed, quietly at first and then almost hysterically. Once again he brushed tears from his eyes, but this time they seemed to be tears of mirth.

"Of course," he said, "I should have known." Sadness replaced his laughter. He shook his head and smiled benevolently, looking from Brown to Barrabas.

"You do not want to know that secret," he said. "It is too terrible. The gold belongs to dead men."

Brother Ulrich moved aside and made for the door to the monastery. Brown blocked his way again.

"The gold is not for me, Ulrich Meser. But we want to know where it is hidden."

Brother Ulrich stopped again and looked at Brown and Barrabas. "If you do not want the gold, then why do you want to know where it is?"

Brown shrugged, a smile playing across his lips. "It's a game. A challenge. To see if we can do it."

The old monk looked thoughtful for a moment, as if he wondered whether to believe the American or not. "We did leave a map, you know," he said finally.

"Where?" Barrabas said impatiently. He felt a sudden urgency that he couldn't explain.

The monk smiled. "There were five of us. We hid the map in the one place where all of us would always be together. It's in Berlin. East or West, I don't know. I have never been back there, and I'm not sure where they put the wall."

"What are you talking about?" Brown said angrily. "Stop playing games and tell us."

"I am trying to warn..."

The monk was interrupted by the sound of running footsteps on the other side of the door into the monastery. Barrabas drew his Jati SMG and grabbed the elderly monk by the arm, dragging him behind the door. Liam O'Toole burst through it and into the garden.

He didn't have time for the flowers.

"Colonel, the Stapo have arrived. Five of them. They just pulled up out front. And they're rushing the place."

Barely had he finished speaking when the sounds of gunfire echoed from the courtyard on the other side of the monastery.

Brother Ulrich began to tremble, his face white with fear. "They are violating the sanctuary."

"Damn right they are," Barrabas snarled. "They're after you, Tom. And how the hell did they know we were here?"

"Don't ask me!" the spy snapped.

Barrabas shook the old monk. "Is there another way out of here?"

"Yes. Yes, there's a gate in the garden wall that leads back to the road. Follow me."

With an agility surprising for a man of his age, the old monk ran into the garden, disappearing into a copse of lilac trees growing along the stone wall.

The two mercs and the CIA agent followed. Set in the wall behind the trees was a gate with a barred door. Brother Ulrich fumbled at the lock with a rusty old key. His hands were weak, and he was unable to turn it. "The lock has rusted."

Barrabas pushed the old man's hand away and grabbed the key. He gritted his teeth and turned. For a moment nothing happened. There were more gunshots from inside the monastery followed by screams.

More gunshots. The screams stopped.

The key turned. Barrabas kicked the gate open. A narrow wooden bridge led across the dank waters of the moat to the tree-lined road.

"Can you put the front door out of commission, O'Toole?" Barrabas asked.

"No problem, sir."

"Good. And take Brother Ulrich. We need some more information from him. I'll stay here and see if I can pick off a few of them from this end and even the odds a little."

The sounds of gunfire grew louder again and they heard shouts in the garden.

"They're here," Brown whispered urgently. "Go!" He grabbed Brother Ulrich by the sleeve, but the old monk pulled away from them.

"No. I will not leave. Never!" He opened his hands in a benediction. "Go in peace, my friends." Then he ran from the cover of the trees back into the garden.

14

Two secret policemen ran through the wooden door and into the garden. They poked through the bushes in the garden with the snouts of their Russian-manufactured autorifles. One of them saw the old monk burst from the cover of the lilac trees. The policemen fired.

Hot geysers of blood spurted across the old man's chest as the bullets hit. The old man froze. He looked at death.

His face contorted, as if it mirrored the expression of each of fifty-six thousand victims. A wind blew through the garden, tossing the flowers as if to awaken them to witness the death of their executioner.

Brother Ulrich belched blood and collapsed, his torn brown habit spreading like a shroud on the earth.

Barrabas went belly down at the edge of the trees. The two German agents ran toward him.

"Go for it!" he ordered O'Toole and Brown.

They ran through the iron door and made their way across the narrow bridge, disappearing into the woods.

Barrabas held the Jati with his right hand ahead of him as he waited on his belly for the first of the two agents to get close enough. He drew a line on the man's forehead. The man was running, and holding his automatic carelessly in front of him. Not watching where he was headed.

Or what was headed for him.

Barrabas.

He fired.

A third eye, the big red one, suddenly winked open in the man's forehead. The back of the skull blew out and blood and brain matter rained down on the flowers. The man bounced up a couple of feet, dropped his rifle and flew back. He came down in the rose garden, spread-eagled and dripping gore. Caught by thorns, the body rocked while a flock of petals flew into the air like tiny pink wings.

One down. One to go.

The second guy was a quick study. He disappeared somewhere in the garden.

Time to hunt.

O'TOOLE AND BROWN ran fast along the road as it wound around the contours of the moat until they came within sight of the front gates of the monastery.

The Mustang was parked where they had left it. But now it was hemmed in between two big black Russian cars. Two men from the Stapo paced on the road and the little drawbridge. Both held submachine guns.

"There must be more of them. That other car wasn't there when I left," O'Toole told Brown. The two men crouched behind a tree. "You have a gun?" the Irish man asked.

"Uh-uh. Hate them," Brown said innocently.

O'Toole was incredulous. "You mean all you have is that little knife?"

"Yeah."

"Sheeesh." O'Toole looked heavenward.

"You didn't see the demo on the train, though," said Brown. "I practice. Watch."

The CIA agent drew the long thin SS dagger from his jacket and held it by the point. He stood, most of his body concealed behind the tree, and waited as one of the German guards approached the other. He stepped out, arm back, one eye closed and threw.

The knife flew like a fluttering silver blur glinting in sunlight.

Whooompf! The guard's head jerked. The knife pierced his temple just above the ear on one side, and the point protruded on the other. The man stood perfectly still and wondered what to do. A tiny sliver of blood dribbled from the wound. His lower jaw dropped, his eyes opened and the white rolled up. Then he fell. Sideways, crumpling over the front fender of the car and sliding off into a heap on the ground, he left a bloody smear on the car. The clatter of his submachine gun onto the road alerted his buddy.

The other guard spun around looking for his missing friend. When he couldn't find him, he panicked. His eyes searched the trees along the road. Thinking the attack had come from there, he darted behind one of the cars and crouched with his back to the moat.

"Now what?" said O'Toole, cocking his handgun. The second guman was clearly visible to them.

"Shoot him," Brown suggested.

"Just like that," O'Toole said sarcastically. "Let's do it a little more quietly. At least until the colonel gets here." From far inside the monastery both men could hear more gunfire.

O'Toole picked up a rock the size of a fist and handed it to Brown. "Are you as good with this as you are with the knife?"

Brown took the rock. "I can try."

"Good. When I'm ready, hit him with it in the back of the head."

The merc picked up a second rock and heaved it overhand past the first car and the Mustang. It hit the second police car's windshield, shattering it into a spiderweb.

The guard spun his head around to look.

"Go!"

Brown stood and pegged the rock as hard as he could.

Straight and narrow. Direct hit.

"Uhgh!" The man grunted as the rock bashed the back of his head in. He tipped forward and fell on his face across the drawbridge.

"Let's go!" O'Toole told Brown. "And keep your eyes open for people on the wall up there." He raced across the open space to the first car with Brown right behind him. He grabbed the submachine gun from the road, where the first dead guard had dropped it and handed it to the spy.

"You know how to use it?"

"Yeah. Sure."

"Then use it if you have to. And keep your eyes up there on the walls in case someone with a gun comes into view."

He ran for the first car and opened the door. The keys were there. He got in and started it up, easing it quickly forward onto the drawbridge. The car hit the body of the second guard and kept going. There was a sickening crunch as the left front tire crushed the man's head. Brain and gore sluiced out across the wooden planks and sprayed into the rank water of the moat.

O'Toole stopped the car and got out. Brown stood by the body of the first dead guard, his SS dagger in hand. The blade was clean.

"How's that going to stop them?" Brown asked.

O'Toole didn't answer. He grabbed the knife from Brown and stabbed it into the front seat of the car, slashing forward as he ripped out a big square of upholstery.

"Open the gas tank," he yelled.

Brown went for it, suddenly grinning. O'Toole had the right idea. He fumbled in his jacket pocket for his cigarette lighter.

BACK IN THE GARDEN, Barrabas scanned the tops of the flowers and shrubs with a cold eye, searching for a certain kind of movement. The tops of the plants swayed slightly in the light breeze. But the breeze was blowing one way, and some bushes about thirty feet to his left were moving the other way.

Barrabas fired off three rounds. The bullets snapped through the dense green foliage, throwing up chips of leaf and twig.

He heard a yelp of pain. The bushes stopped moving. But that was no guarantee.

A songbird screeched with alarm from some nearby bushes and took sudden flight. Barrabas rolled fast on the grass into a flower bed as the German police agent stood up from behind the hedgerow a dozen feet off.

He was covered with blood and his face showed he'd had a glimpse of hell. But his aim was still accurate. Rounds of 7.62 mm heavy bullets chewed the earth, splashing Barrabas with grit. He stopped, lay on his back feeling the thorns press into him and a sudden pain across the side of his head. He pushed himself up, fell back on his elbow and fired off the Jati in his left hand.

The gun chat-a-chat-chatted, blowing away the man's face and sending him flat into the bushes like a punch-up doll. The colonel jumped up and went for the exit gate just as three more Stapo heavies ran from the monastery into the garden.

A time to fight and a time to run.

This time was for running.

He slammed the iron-barred gate behind him, reached through and pulled out the key. He locked the gate and threw the key into the moat.

Barrabas rounded the monastery and saw the moat just as the big Russian car blew into a column of orange flame twenty feet high. He could feel the heat punch into him as blackened debris sailed high over his head and splashed into the moat. Flames licked up against the outer stone wall of the monastery. The front door was now completely blocked.

O'Toole ran back up the gravel road just as Barrabas came out of cover.

He panted to catch his breath. "Colonel, just coming back to give you a hand."

"It's taken care of. Let's get the hell out of here."

Both men ran for the Mustang, where Tom Brown waited for them behind the wheel. O'Toole stopped by the side of the second Stapo car and lit the rags stuffed into its gas tank. The flames caught. The Mustang was moving. Barrabas and O'Toole jumped over the sides into the seats. Brown floored it and the car spun away in a cloud of gravel dust.

He booted it down the hillside on the winding road with two fingers on the wheel and the eager smile of a daredevil who knew his car. Just as the monastery disappeared from sight, Barrabas looked back.

The flames of the burning car were lower now as toxic black smoke from burning rubber and plastic billowed into the air.

There was movement at the gates of the monastery as men tried to get around the burning wreck. But that wasn't what caused the chill that crawled at the back of the colonel's neck.

On the walls, a tall woman with long blond hair watched impassively as the turquoise Mustang disappeared down the hill. She held her hands out in front of her, with the fingers spread apart like fans. They were almost supernaturally long. And the edges glinted in the sunlight. She would let them go, she thought to herself, and arrange for their crossing into the West to be uncomplicated. Then they would be hers.

NOT MUCH LATER, Brown squealed the Mustang onto the main road with a whoop of victory.

"We sure beat our asses out of there!" he cried gleefully, booting the car up the highway. "Whoooo-pieee!"

"Brown!" Barrabas yelled against the wind. "Brooowwn! What are you so happy about? The old man didn't tell us dick all."

"Uh-uh, Nile. The old man said enough. He told us how to find the gold."

The CIA man smiled and whooped again. "Back to Berlin!" he cried.

O'Toole leaned close to Barrabas and spoke barely loud enough for the colonel to hear. "I think I want to bust his legs." He motioned toward Tom Brown.

"Yes sirreee!" the American spy crowed. "We're on the trail of Nazi gold!" He noticed that the two mercs weren't sharing his glee.

"Mind filling us in?" Barrabas said coolly.

"Why sure. He said there was a map and that we'd find it in the one place where all five members of his SS group were always together. In Berlin."

"So what did that mean?"

Brown was still grinning. "There's only one place in the world he could mean. The Nazi Documentation Center in West Berlin. It's the nine million files from the Nazi Party Headquarters that the Allies seized after the war. And it includes the army records of every member of the SS, as well. It's in the American sector, in West Berlin. I'll bet you a hundred million dollars' worth of Nazi gold that if we dig up the military records of the *Gruppe*, we'll find the map."

"Brother Ulrich also said it belonged to dead men. What'd he mean by that?"

Brown shrugged. "Who knows?" He pressed harder on the gas and the Mustang tore along the East German highway.

Somehow, Barrabas thought, they were going to get more than any of them had bargained for.

15

The Nazi Documentation Center was located in a three-story stone building on an isolated part of the Landeswehr Kanal, not far from the Wall in West Berlin. The front doors faced the street that ran along the water. A driveway at the side led to a parking lot behind the Center.

In the front foyer, a security guard sat to one side bouncing a handful of keys idly in one hand. He was not looking forward to the long graveyard shift that stretched ahead. The building had been closed to the public, and he had just finished locking up.

Stairs led from the foyer to a balcony, where another set of doors opened into the main reading room. A second security guard thumbed through a magazine. One side of the large hall was taken up by rows of bookshelves, holding file boxes heavy with documents seized by the American and Russian armies from the Nazi headquarters in 1945. In the center of the room a half-dozen scholars worked late, reading material at big oak tables. On the other wide, several librarians sat at their desks or flipped through filing cabinets.

It was quiet, peaceful—and the wrong place at the wrong time.

Two black Mercedes drove down the street along the Landeswehr Kanal and slowed to a stop near the front doors of the Documentation Center. The driver of the first car, Ernst Krankenkor, Sturmbannführer of the Bitburg Patriotic Group, turned to Karl Haupt, who sat in the passenger seat beside him.

"It is five-thirty. You are certain the building will be almost empty?"

Haupt nodded. "In the evenings there is only a small skeleton staff and security guards. No one to be concerned about."

Krankenkor nodded. He turned and looked at Uwe, the soccer champion, who sat in the back seat. "You know what to do?"

"Yes, of course," the tall blond storm trooper snarled. "Have I not spent the last twenty-four hours studying the plans our friend Herr Haupt brought us?" He pulled the Schmeisser from under the seat and patted it. A silencer had been attached to the barrel. "I know exactly what must be done. The American army of occupation must be driven from the fatherland. I will show no mercy."

Haupt pointed to a bridge a little farther up the road. "We shall cross the canal there and wait. You have half an hour to eliminate the opposition and bring us the necessary papers."

"Sieg heil!" Uwe folded the metal stock of the SMG and inserted it under his jacket. He wedged the butt into his armpit to conceal it completely.

Uwe left the car and walked to the second Mercedes, which had pulled up behind. He tapped on the window. Gunther, Axel and Dietmar opened the doors. Wolfgang stayed at the wheel. The four young Nazis waited outside the front doors as the two Mercedes pulled away from the curb and turned onto the bridge. Uwe reached into his pocket and pulled out a handful of blood-red armbands, which bore black swastikas in white circles. The young men pulled them on.

Uwe nodded at Axel and Dietmar. "Take the entrance at the rear. We will meet you inside."

The two young men walked toward the back of the building. Uwe and Gunther waited a moment outside the front entrance. Then Uwe rang the bell.

After what seemed like a long wait, an elderly security guard stopped in front of the doors. He waved his arms at the two men, telling them to go away.

Uwe shook his head and pounded his fist on the door. The guard walked closer and inserted a key in the lock. He pulled the door open a few inches.

"We are closed," he said crankily. "Come back tomor—"

He was cut off by the barrel of the Schmeisser that Uwe slipped from his jacket and rammed into his guts. The Schmeisser vibrated as a half-dozen rounds of 9 mm parabellum slammed into the old man. He looked momentarily surprised, his eyes gazing into the blond German's. He slumped forward against the door. Uwe reached inside and pushed the man back. The guard flopped onto the floor.

The two men pushed into the building and slammed the door behind them. Uwe locked it. "Drag the body there," he told Gunther, pointing to a corner away from the doors.

Gunther grabbed the body by the arms and began to drag it. The floor was slippery with blood. Uwe helped him. When they were finished, Gunther was shaking.

"You are nervous," Uwe accused him coldly.

"Nein, nein!" Gunther protested. "It's just . . . my first time. I've never seen—"

"Always remember we do this for the fatherland."

"*Jawohl*, Uwe." Gunther stiffened, pulling himself together.

"Come." Uwe galloped up the steps to the first floor and burst through the doors into the main reading room.

The startled librarians and scholars looked up from their work as the two men strode into the room.

"Freeze! All of you!" Uwe shouted, leveling his SMG.

"But, we are closed—" the second security guard began.

"Go for it, Gunther," Uwe ordered.

Gunther pointed his Schmeisser and fired.

The guard bucked as the bullets plowed through his face. His chair tipped back and the magazine fell to the floor. For a moment the chair teetered on its back legs. Uwe aimed and fired a single round into the guard's chest. Guard and chair flew back and thudded onto the floor.

A short plump woman murmured "Oh my God!" over and over as the others stood in horrified silence. Dietmar and Axel burst through an exit at the side of the room behind the stacks of bookshelves and fanned out along the other side of the room.

"No noise!" Uwe shouted at the panic-stricken people. "You will all gather there!" With the barrel of his rifle he pointed to where the plump woman stood.

The five hostages, their eyes wide with fear, did as they were told. One of the scholars took off his glasses, wiped them on his sleeve and addressed the young Nazis.

"Now please, stay calm," he said. "I don't know what you want, but whatever it is, take it. We won't cause any trouble."

Uwe grinned. "No, you won't cause trouble. Gunther! Axel! Dietmar! Come here!"

The four teammates stood in a row facing the horrified academics.

"You!" Uwe pointed at the man with the glasses. "Come here and kneel at my feet."

The man swallowed and slowly approached Uwe. He knelt in front of the young man. Uwe placed the barrel of his SMG against the man's forehead. "Are there any more people in the building?" he demanded.

"N-no!" the man cried desperately.

Uwe looked at the other prisoners. One of the women had buried her face in the chest of a thin elderly man with gray hair. All the hostages shook their heads anxiously.

"Fine." Uwe took his gun away. "You can stand with your friends." The scholar stood and walked back to the others, visibly relieved. Uwe turned to Dietmar and Axel.

"The files are upstairs. Take the fat woman. She will find the papers we need."

Axel strode forward and grabbed the plump woman by her wrist. She pulled back, protesting. "No. Please!"

Axel slapped her hard across the face. One of the men jumped forward to stop him. Axel turned with the butt of his gun and slammed it into the man's stomach. The man went down with a grunt of pain.

Axel kicked him back into line, where he squirmed in agony at the feet of his friends.

The fat woman began to weep.

"Go!" Uwe commanded his cohorts. Dietmar and Axel pushed the woman through the office and disappeared up the steps to the second floor.

Uwe waited patiently until they were gone. Then he turned to Gunther.

"On three."

Gunther nodded. The two Nazi youths faced the hostages with their SMGs staring like eyeballs from hell.

"One. Two..."

The prisoners started to scream.

"Three."

Clenching hard on the Schmeissers, Uwe and Gunther mowed rounds of bullets back and forth into the lineup of innocents, zippering their bodies with explosions of blood and gore. The hostages danced backward. Their bodies jerked and tumbled down. A sheet of gore spattered onto the floor and furniture. Uwe and Gunter fired until their mags were empty.

The room was suddenly quiet again.

"For the fatherland," Uwe murmured. He smiled at Gunther. *"Es geht?"* he asked. "Are you all right?"

Gunter nodded. His face was white.

IT WAS EARLY EVENING when Barrabas and O'Toole pulled up outside the Nazi Documentation Center in a lonely part of downtown West Berlin. The border crossing at Checkpoint Charlie hadn't been as hard as they'd thought it would be. In fact, it was almost too easy.

Tom Brown turned off the lights of the Mustang.

"It's closed," he said.

"Let's try to talk our way past the night staff," Barrabas suggested.

"Can't hurt to try," O'Toole said. The three men's eyes met in silent agreement.

The street outside was deserted. In the distance traffic swept up a busier street. Two cars were parked on a small bridge across the canal, not far away.

The three Americans walked up the steps to the front door of the building. The brass plaque identifying the building was so small and discreet it was almost unnoticeable. Overhead, cords on four naked flagpoles clattered in the growing breeze.

The doors into the marble entrance lobby were locked. No one was in sight. Brown looked around for the bell to summon the security staff.

"Colonel," O'Toole called. He stood next to the doors, looking inside the lobby. "Over to the far left, sir."

Barrabas stood beside him and looked in. The floor was covered with a shiny red slick.

"Don't push it!" Barrabas snapped at Brown just as the CIA man found the bell.

From far inside the building they heard something—the stuttering pops of silenced autofire.

DIETMAR AND AXEL pounded down the steps and burst into the reading room, waving the files they had found upstairs.

"We killed the old bitch," Dietmar commented, glancing at the pile of corpses.

"Axel, watch the door," Uwe ordered. He took the files and set them on a table. There were five of them.

Uwe quickly flipped through each, knowing exactly what to look for.

He withdrew the identity cards. The faces of young Nazi warriors, the five men who had made up the company under Captain Ulrich Meser's command, stared out from the yellowed photographs. Uwe flipped the cards over.

"There it is!" he cried to the other neo-Nazis who had crowded around. Arranged in a square, four of the cards formed a map of Berlin. A place near Potsdamerplatz that marked the sight of Hitler's Chancellery was in the center. Radiating from it were lines marking the subways and streets. A square had been drawn around the part of the map showing the Chancellery and the nearby streets. Uwe threw the fifth card onto the table. It was a detailed inset of the square.

"Look!" Uwe said triumphantly to the others with a great smile. "Can you imagine a more brilliant hiding place. We have been chosen as the successors of the Third Reich. Tonight we shall collect our inheritance. To do so, we have only to penetrate the lair of the *Führer* himself!"

OUTSIDE, LIAM O'TOOLE worked feverishly, squeezing a wad of plastic explosive into the crack where the lock mechanism held the doors closed. Barrabas handed him the fuse, which he pressed into the soft putty. Both men darted to shelter on either side of the doors, out of the blast line. Tom Brown was waiting on one side with the detonator in his hand. On signal, he pressed it.

The plastics blew almost instantaneously, sending a burst of smoke and bits of glass and torn metal flying.

The two mercs whipped their Jatis from the shoulder holsters and pivoted through the broken doors.

They spun in an arc across the lobby, firing double 3-round bursts to discourage any welcoming party. There was no one. The bloody body of the security guard lay in a corner.

Barrabas looked up the steps to the door that led into the main reading room. The startled face of a young man looked down at them. He carried a rifle, slung over his shoulder and pointing uselessly at the ceiling.

Barrabas swept his arm around, peered straight down the sights of the Jati to the man's forehead. He fired once.

Axel turned to flee just as the bullet hit. He kept spinning, his head a bloody centrifuge.

Barrabas took the stairs three and four at a time, with O'Toole behind him. Tom Brown entered the building, quickly looking around to see where the guns were. The two mercs neared the top of the stairs just as Axel fell limply over the railing and landed on the floor at Brown's feet. The top of his head was blown open. But that wasn't what caught the CIA agent's attention. It was the swastika arm band around the dead man's sleeve.

"Holy shit," Brown muttered. "How in hell did they know about this?"

He kicked the body aside and ran after Barrabas.

UWE AND FRIENDS HEARD the autofire echo through the lobby. They looked up in time to see Axel's brains splatter against the office doors. Their buddy spun over the edge of the balcony and disappeared.

"We are under attack!" Uwe shouted. He snatched the cards from the table and shoved them into one of the files. Clenching it under his arm, he grabbed his Schmeisser and set a long wasteful stream of bullets at the door. Jagged chunks of glass blew outside. Dietmar and Gunther clutched their guns and looked at their leader, wondering what to do.

"We go out the back door!" Uwe shouted. "Go!" He waved them ahead. The three men tore down the center of the room just as Barrabas and O'Toole burst through the broken doors.

The pile of dead bodies told the tale. Barrabas rained hard autofire at the fleeting killers as they took cover behind a table. Uwe threw a savage tirade of bullets back. The two mercs jumped behind the bookcase nearest the doors. Barrabas saw Tom Brown at the top of the stairs, just about to enter the main hall. He shook his gun urgently, warning him back.

Across the room, a long oak table went over on its side, and the young Nazis crowded behind it, using it as a barricade. Dietmar sat the snout of his Schmeisser on the edge of the table and fired at the stacks that hid Barrabas and O'Toole. The bullets pounded harmlessly into wood and paper. O'Toole put one hand around the side of the bookshelves—the hand with the Jati. He peered through the stacks, guesstimated and fired. One of the three bullets hit the edge of the wooden table. Dietmar screamed and disappeared.

Behind the table, Dietmar was scared but unhurt. He and Gunther looked to Uwe for instructions.

"We must make a run for the back door," Uwe said, pointing to the Exit sign that hung on the wall on the far side of the stacks. They had to cross twenty feet of open space before they got to the shelter of the bookshelves. "Gunther, you will give us cover," Uwe ordered.

"Me?" Gunther asked weakly.

"*Ja.* You. Then we will cover for you. Ready?"

Gunter swallowed. This was more than he had bargained for—a lot harder than clubbing or shooting defenceless people to death. Uwe nailed him with a cold stare. Reluctantly, Gunther nodded.

Uwe and Dietmar crowded together at the end of the table, preparing to make a run for it. Gunther put the barrel of his Schmeisser on the edge of the overturned table. Not daring to raise his head, he aimed toward the front doors where he hoped the intruders were. He closed his eyes, crossed his fingers and squeezed the trigger.

IN THE DARKNESS of their car, on the bridge outside the Documentation Center, Krankenkor and Haupt saw the turquoise Mustang pull up in front.

"Barrabas," Haupt hissed when the mercs left the car.

"Who," Krankenkor asked urgently.

Haupt looked at him, his eyes narrowed."Never mind. You don't know him. I do. You must call this off. All of it. Now."

"That is impossible. My storm troopers will take care of these intruders!"

Haupt laughed, too loud to conceal his sudden anxiety. "Fool! Veteran assassins have tried to eliminate this man and failed. He is my greatest enemy. Your operation is over, Krankenkor. Someone has betrayed you."

"Impossible!" Krankenkor shouted, his eyes bulging in anger. "We will go in after them to help the storm troopers!" He reached over the seat, grabbing the Schmeisser that lay hidden on the floor in the back.

"Don't bother," Haupt said coldly. Krankenkor heard the chilling metal click of a gun. He stopped and looked at Haupt. Then he looked at the small M-50 in Haupt's hand.

"Put that away!" Krankenkor snarled. "Nothing can stop us!" He pulled the Schmeisser into the front seat. "Nothing!"

Except a bullet. Haupt fired. The bullets slammed into Krankenkor's heart, pushing him against the door. He looked at Haupt, a silent question in his eyes. He would never ask it now.

Haupt reached past the body and pulled the door handle. As the door swung open, Haupt gave the body a solid push with his foot and kicked it outside. It flopped onto the pavement as he climbed behind the wheel.

Karl Haupt had come up against Barrabas before and there was nothing he'd like better than to off the warrior once and for all.

But he knew better than to underestimate the man. The car spun away from the bridge and headed for downtown Berlin. Someday, thought Haupt, Barrabas would get his. But not from these amateur neo-Nazis.

Meanwhile, in the second Mercedes on the bridge, Wolfgang stared at the quickly departing car with his mouth open and his eyes wide. He looked at the body lying on the bridge where the car had been parked. Then he looked back at the Documentation Center.

The American car was still there, but those who had arrived in it were nowhere in sight. The front doors of the building were shattered and swung crazily on broken hinges. Now another big black car, with East German license plates, was pulling into the driveway that led to the parking lot behind the building.

Wolfgang didn't know what was going on, but he knew it wasn't part of the plan. He opened the door and ran to the body on the road. It was Krankenkor, his chest soaked in blood. Dead.

"Mein Gott!" Wolfgang exclaimed. He ran for his car. Uwe and the others were still inside the building. He spun the car around in a U-turn and raced back to save his Nazi buddies.

As the big East German car pulled into the parking lot, Ilsa spoke to the three big Stapo officers who accompanied her. One drove. The other two were in the back seat.

"The American spy's car is here. He must be inside. Now that we know what he is after, he can be killed. Along with the two men who accompany him."

The driver pulled over and stopped the car, as the other men inserted 40-round mags into their silenced, Czeck Model 25s. Ilsa unwrapped a leather roll and snapped the long deadly razors onto each of her fingers.

"You will cover the front entrance," she said to the big Stapo killer beside her. Then she looked at the two men in the back seat. "You will both come with me. I will rely on you to slow down anyone who tries to run past us." The sharp deadly nails on each finger glinted as she waved her hands.

"But, if possible, leave the final touch to me."

16

Inside the Documentation Center there was momentary calm as Barrabas and O'Toole waited for some action from their Nazi opponents.

"There's another exit over there," Barrabas said to O'Toole. He pointed to the aisle that led between the rows of bookshelves and the wall. "My guess is they'll make a run for it. You give them some fire here. If they pin you down and try to run for it, I'll be at the other end of the stack."

He ran quickly and silently along the narrow aisle between the high bookshelves until he came to the end of the row. The aisle that ran along the wall afforded a clear view of the exit door. The door was centered in the wall; there were six rows of bookshelves in either direction. The aisle in between was no man's land.

A stream of autofire broke from behind the table. Bullets pounded madly into the wall over O'Toole's head as the Irish American darted behind the cover of the bookshelf. Clouds of plaster rained on him. The bullets went far and wide, chewing into papers and books scattered on the tables and desks.

O'Toole fired off a 3-round burst one-handed with the Jati. The enemy fire stopped. He held up two fingers for Barrabas and pointed to the wall. Two men had made a run for it.

Barrabas nodded. He jumped into the aisle holding his SMG steady with both hands and fired on full-auto as Uwe and Dietmar came to the end of the stacks. They appeared briefly in the aisle. One of them yelped, dropped his rifle and jumped back, pushing the other ahead of him. A hand reached from the stacks and grabbed for the fallen rifle. Barrabas let off a quick 3-round burst that kicked into the floor. The hand pulled out. The rifle stayed where it was.

Now it was time to flush them out. Cat-and-mouse style.

TOM BROWN KEPT HIS BACK against the wall outside the main reading room, until the two men made a run for the stacks from behind their barricade. When O'Toole returned fire, driving the last rifleman behind cover of the table, Brown took his chance.

He kept low, swinging around the door and running for cover of the desk near the pile of corpses. As he went, he saw the files spread open on a table in the center of the room. They were chewed up by bullets, but they were unquestionably SS files. The Nazis had got there first.

Across the room, O'Toole and Barrabas were darting between the rows of bookshelves, moving along the stacks toward their cornered quarry. They seemed to not have noticed Brown. The room was momentarily quiet again.

Brown crab-walked among the desks toward the back of the room, where the gunman hid behind the overturned table. He peered around the side of the last desk. The gunman was barely ten feet away. Two more Nazis cowered behind the bookshelves, eyeing the side exit. One of them had a file under his arm. Brown knew he had to get it.

He slipped his dagger from his jacket and held it securely in his right fist, thumb on the hilt. He peered around the edge of the desk again. Gunther's back was turned to him. He was communicating silently with his two companions. On signal, Gunther raised the barrel of his submachine gun and fired over the table. Uwe and Dietmar splashed bullets down the far aisle and ran toward the door. Barrabas answered with return fire. The two Nazis ducked behind the next row of shelves for cover.

Brown swung around the desk and ran for Gunther. The young Nazi saw him coming from the corner of his eye, just as he pulled the Schmeisser away and ducked. Too late.

The CIA man's hand swooped down over Gunther's face and jerked his head back. The knife in Brown's fist swung like a sledgehammer from his powerful shoulder. The sharp point of the knife pierced Gunther's skull and melted through to the brain. Brown plunged it to the hilt. The point protruded a sixteenth of an inch out of the underside of Gunther's chin. Death was instantaneous. Brown felt the life drain from the body like water bursting through a wet paper bag.

Uwe and Dietmar turned and saw their buddy die. Uwe aimed his Schmeisser at Brown and pressed the trigger.

Brown was ready for it.

He clenched the limp body by the back of the shirt and used it for a shield. The lead punching into Gunther knocked him back, but the 9 mm bullets didn't pierce the corpse.

Brown hoisted Gunther to his feet and ran straight for Uwe and Dietmar, holding the body in front of him. The two Nazis stared, horrified, as the lifeless body of their comrade rushed them. Dietmar ran for the end of the stack and no man's land. Uwe kept firing, backing toward the wall and Barrabas's line of fire.

Liam O'Toole saw Brown dart from the desk and disappear behind the table. Suddenly the scattered covering fire from behind the barricade stopped. The next thing O'Toole knew, the crazy spy was hurtling forward with the body of the gunman in front of him, in a suicidal assault on the other two men hidden in the stacks.

"Brown's got him! They're making a run for it!" he shouted to Barrabas. The white-haired soldier whipped around the corner, sending a line of autofire up the aisle to keep the escaping Nazis pinned away from the exit door.

Suddenly the door opened from the other side. Two burly men burst through, firing machine pistols in each direction. Barrabas felt a bullet chip his left forearm as he pulled back behind the bookshelves. He fired off a few last rounds to empty the mag. He wiped the blood from his hand and grabbed another mag from his pocket.

"We got company, O'Toole!" he called, looking back for the sargeant. O'Toole was gone.

While Barrabas slicked down the aisle from the end of the bookshelves with his Jati, O'Toole darted from cover and ran up the aisle between the bookshelves. He blasted autofire into the side aisles as a precaution while he made for the row where the two neo-Nazi storm troopers were hidden. He had barely arrived at the middle row, which gave him a clear view to the exit, when the door opened.

Two big men in dark coats burst into the room. They fired as they came. O'Toole swung himself forward behind the cover of the next bookshelf as double fists punched into his chest on the left side.

Those weren't fists. They were bullets. He was bleeding. But it was no time to stop. O'Toole raced for the row that hid Tom Brown.

Brown had thrown Gunther's body like a rag doll as Uwe emptied his Schmeisser at it.

Click. No more bullets.

The body fell heavily on top of the storm trooper, knocking him to the floor. The Schmeisser and the file of papers fell from his hands. He rolled over, scrambling to pull himself out from under the corpse.

Brown threw himself at Uwe, clenching the man's ankle with an iron grip and holding him down. The spy's hands crawled up the storm trooper's legs, clutching his flesh, hand over hand. Uwe howled and kicked.

Brown caught a heavy boot in the jaw that threw him off. He heard Barrabas shout, and a heavy burst of machine-gun fire came from the middle of the stacks. Uwe twisted and pulled his leg away. He sprang to his feet and into the aisle after Dietmar.

The exit door was wide open. Through the little window in the door, he could see the white-haired colonel blowing off rounds into the aisle. The glass smashed but the solid wood door shielded the two fleeing men from the bullets. Dietmar raced through, his heavy boots clattering on the metal stairs as the door closed behind him.

Uwe ran for it.

Another man, wearing a dark overcoat, aimed a machine pistol around the corner of one of the bookshelves at Barrabas. The American ducked behind the stacks just as Uwe slid down the aisle and pushed through the narrow opening onto the metal stairs. The doors closed behind him. He ran as if his life depended on it. It did.

Brown scrambled at the sheets of papers that had spilled out of Uwe's file, grabbing and thrusting the documents into his pockets. A sudden burst of autofire heralded O'Toole's arrival between the stacks of books. The merc's jacket was torn, the cloth stained with blood.

"Two big mothers just walked in from nowhere!" he muttered urgently, taking up position so he could fire down the room.

Brown grabbed the knife protruding from the head of dead Gunther. It didn't budge. He put his foot against it for leverage and pulled. Slowly it emerged from the man's head. A small quantity of blood followed. Brown wiped the blade on the dead man's sleeve.

A sudden silence filled the Documentation Center. The main reading room was a slaughter field. No one moved.

"Where are they?" Brown whispered to O'Toole.

"Middle row. About six up."

Brown motioned for O'Toole to come closer. "Let's see if we can move this," he whispered into the merc's ear, and pointed to the bookshelf that shielded them from the killers. The two men put their shoulders to the seven-foot-tall stack and shoved, slowly, pressing their combined weights against it. It tipped. Just a little, but enough.

The two men shifted their weight to hold the bookshelf steady. O'Toole felt the ripples of pain burst through his chest from the left side. The bullets had grazed his side and torn open the skin. Maybe a couple of ribs were broken, but nothing was punctured. It hurt like hell.

"Hey, Barrabas!" Brown's voice rang out foolishly loud in the silent room. The sounds of magazines abruptly snapped into the Stapo agents' machine pistols answered from the middle row.

"Yeah! I hear you!" Barrabas answered Brown's call from his position behind the bookshelves near the front door.

"Hear the one about the flat-chested woman's libber?" Brown called. He gave O'Toole a signal and the two men put their weight against the bookshelves again. "She burned her bra—and her stack fell," Brown shouted the last two words. They shoved hard into the bookshelf. It started to tip.

DIETMAR AND UWE clattered down the metal stairs to the outside parking lot. Dietmar had a head start. He came to the fire door at the bottom and ran.

Smack into a nightmare.

Ilsa was waiting.

The Stapo she-wolf's arm reached out and swept wide, the razor-tipped fingers swiping smoothly across Dietmar's stomach. The deadly nails shredded the young man's midsection, splitting it open in five straight slits. Dietmar's guts tumbled out onto the pavement. The young Nazi looked at them lying on the ground outside his body. The world was silent and moving very slowly. He looked up at Ilsa.

"Those are mine," he said clearly. He meant the guts.

Ilsa glared at the disemboweled storm trooper and readied her arm again. It hurtled forward, the blades glinting sharply.

She sliced a long shallow line across Dietmar's shocked face, then swooped down with a backhand. Ticktacktoe. The blood started. His face became a red mask.

Uwe came to the foot of the stairs just as Ilsa finished. The attack by the Bitburg Patriotic Group had already turned from retreat into full rout. It was 1945 all over again. But when Uwe saw Ilsa and what was left of Dietmar, he went from running to hiding. He ducked into the darkness behind the stairs just as Ilsa opened the door and ran into the building.

When the Stapo officer disappeared up the stairs, Uwe made his run for it. He slipped outside and froze—face to bloody face with Dietmar. The Bitburg buddy looked like a fountain carved from blood. He groaned lowly, as if even his scream had been torn from him. He rocked unsteadily on his feet, anchored by the line of slimy intestines and blinded faceless by his own blood.

A car screeched into the driveway, the lights dazing Uwe. It pulled alongside. The tires screeched as Wolfgang braked in front of the tall blond Nazi leader. Uwe backed away from Dietmar in horror. He jumped in the car, and the two Nazi youths drove quickly away.

WHEN THE ROOM STARTED TO MOVE, so did Barrabas. Brown's joke was bad, but the lousy punch line told him what was coming. Being crushed under a ton of books was not his idea of a good time. He scrambled toward the front door of the reading room as O'Toole and Brown stepped out at the other end.

The bookshelves went over one by one like giant dominoes. The two Stapo gunmen heard the thunder and felt the room shake. Then they realized it was all about to fall on them. They tried to run. An arm and a leg appeared in the middle row when the case in front of it went over. The scream that emerged was full of sinking awareness. It was strangled abruptly. As rows of heavy bookshelves toppled, thousands of books and file boxes fell, crushing the Stapo gunmen. There was feeble motion among the debris and then there was only stillness.

Brown and O'Toole ran down the room while Barrabas covered them from the front door. When the two men went past him, he turned to follow them.

O'Toole saw another big goon at the bottom of the stairs. He slammed full-auto rounds into him. The big killer smacked sideways and sagged to the floor.

The three Americans pounded down the stairs and out the front doors of the Documentation Center.

"We got it!" Brown shrieked as they hit the summer air outside. Barrabas and O'Toole didn't stop. They jumped sideways off the front steps and ran to the side of the building to see what the opposition was like.

It was a horror show.

What was left of Dietmar was, incredibly, still standing, anchored to his mound of wet intestines and wondering whether to die or not. The monster rocked back and forth, groaning awesomely. Barrabas lobbed a couple of rounds into the ghoul's head. Brain death. But Dietmar's body refused to die. He lurched back, his grisly umbilicus pulling at the pile of guts on the ground. Barrabas fired again. This time the bullet sliced the long intestinal rope leading from Dietmar's open belly. The Nazi quivered briefly and fell.

The turquoise Mustang came at Barrabas and O'Toole across the grass, full speed in reverse. It braked sharply, digging into the ground and sending up clumps of earth as the two mercs jumped in. Tom Brown slammed it into forward and tore into the street.

A few minutes later, with several kilometers between them and the field of battle, Brown pulled over on a dark quiet boulevard deep in the Tiergarten.

"Who the hell were all those people?" O'Toole roared.

"The big guys were Stapo. From East Germany," Brown said.

"How in hell did they know where to find you?" Barrabas demanded.

"And those men with the swastikas?" O'Toole asked.

Brown shrugged. "It looks like we're not the only ones going after Nazi gold," he replied.

"And who cut up that guy back there?" Barrabas looked at Brown. The CIA man didn't know what he meant. He described Dietmar.

"Phew!" Brown responded with an anxious sigh. "Ilsa."

Barrabas waited for further explanation.

"She's a legend in the Stapo," said Brown. "A blond woman, said to be very beautiful, and one of their best agents. Her favored weapons are razor blades. It had to be her."

"It was," Barrabas said. "I saw her."

O'Toole and Brown looked at the mercenary commander.

"At the monastery just as we pulled out, and just now at the Documentation Center when the last of the shelves went over and I was covering you two. The exit door opened. I saw her standing there for a second. A blond woman with . . ." He paused.

"Say it," Brown said, knowing full well what was coming.

"Say what?" O'Toole was puzzled.

"Fingernails eight inches long." Barrabas sounded as if he didn't believe his own words.

Brown nodded. "That's what the stories about her say."

"Well, it looks to me that with those neo-Nazis and the Stapo, we are between a rock and a hard place," the colonel commented.

"Yup," Brown said happily. "But we have something they don't." He reached into his pocket and pulled out a messy sheaf of papers. "The map."

17

Brown pulled up in front of the Berlin hotel where Barrabas and O'Toole had set up earlier that day. The doormen took their car. As the three men walked into the modern lobby, Brown bounced along, straining to contain his excitement.

Barrabas figured Brown's success as a CIA agent and spy had been due as much to good luck as to genuine prowess. Some people could pull it off that way. But Barrabas and O'Toole were trained fighters. As soon as they entered the hotel, their eyes quick-scanned the room, noting the people, exits and elevators.

They stopped and looked at each other.

"Did you hear what I heard?" O'Toole asked in disbelief.

Barrabas nodded. "In the bar."

They crossed the lobby and walked into the lounge just as Alex Nanos pulled up his sleeve, bent his arm and clenched his fist. The bicep on his right arm swelled to enormous proportions.

"That's the way they make us in California, *Fräulein*," he told a mesmerized Germanic beauty with plaited blond hair.

"*Ja!* So big!" She giggled.

"That's not all that's big, baby..."

"Schnapps!" Nate Beck announced, returning from the bar bearing two small glasses of clear liquid. He handed one to the Greek, but his eyes were glued to the *Fräulein*. He seemed as enamored as Nanos. Or else he was just supplying the competition. Nanos never liked the game to be too easy.

They chinked their glasses and raised them to drink. Two thick arms reached from behind them and grabbed the glasses from their hands.

"You're on duty now, boys!" O'Toole bellowed when the two mercs whipped around. He held the schnapps. Colonel Barrabas was smiling at his two soldiers.

"Excuse," O'Toole said. He reached past Nanos and Beck and handed a glass of schnapps to Heidi. "*Fräulein*, please."

She took it graciously. "*Danke schön*. Cheers!" She giggled again and gulped it back. Her cheeks became even rosier.

Tom Brown arrived in the lounge. He looked over Nanos and Beck with curiosity and automatically reached for the second glass of schnapps in O'Toole's hand. He gulped it down.

"Oooof!" Brown choked on the peppermint-flavored liquid. "This stuff's awful!"

"Alex, Nate, this is Tom Brown, the... man I told you about," Barrabas introduced them. "Tom, we call Alex 'the Greek' sometimes. A good fighting man. And Nate Beck is our electronics and tech expert."

"We got your call, Colonel, so here we are," Nanos said. "Right, Nate!" He slapped his buddy on the back.

"You called these guys," O'Toole asked the colonel in disbelief.

Barrabas nodded. "Before we left Amsterdam. These little jobs for Walker Jessup usually turn into big ones."

"Sure, Sarge," Nanos burst out. "And it was a chance to give you a second send-off to married life."

"Well, a send-off would be one thing, boys," O'Toole told them. "But if the colonel called you, that means you were drinking on assignment. Two thousand dollars fine for each of you, off your next paycheck."

Nanos and Beck looked horrified.

"But, Sarge, it was just..." Beck started.

"Forget it, guys," O'Toole said gruffly. "Forget the booze, forget the *Fräulein* and get upstairs."

The two mercs looked at their leader, making a last plea for clemency.

"What about him?" Nanos said weakly, pointing at Tom Brown, who was wiping the taste of the schnapps from his lips with the back of his hand.

"He works for himself, not for me," Barrabas said, supporting O'Toole as his second in command. "It's his suicide."

"Auf Widersehen, Fräulein," Nanos said to the woman.

"Tchüss!" she giggled, and threw them a little wave.

"Oh man, did you see those thighs," Nate said longingly as the mercs left the lounge.

Nanos sighed.

NOT FAR FROM THE HOTEL, in Krankenkor's Kreuzberg apartment, the candles under the portrait of Adolf Hitler were lit once again.

But Krankenkor wasn't there. His dead body was sprawled on the bridge near the Nazi Documentation Center. The last two remaining members of the Bitburg Patriotic Group talked anxiously.

"You are sure it was Sturmbannführer Krankenkor who fell dead from the car?" Uwe demanded.

"Yes, absolutely." Wolfgang answered his leader. "And then this American man, Haupt, drove away."

Uwe clenched his fist and pounded on the arm of the chair. "A traitor in our midst! We will spare nothing to find him and liquidate him."

"But, Uwe," Wolfgang gulped nervously, "who are these other people? And what was the terrible thing that happened to Dietmar? I saw..." His voice broke as he recalled the horror.

"I don't know." The tall blond storm trooper stood up and paced.

"But there are others now, also after the gold that our Nazi forefathers left for us." Wolfgang wrung his hands nervously.

"Ja!" Uwe cried, turning toward Wolfgang and leaning over him. "So we must move quickly to get to it first!"

Wolfgang pressed back in the chair and took a deep breath. Uwe's gaze pierced through him. He summoned his inner strength and answered calmly.

"But they have the map."

Uwe straightened and slowly smiled. "But they do not have all of it." He held up one of the identity cards that he had taken from the SS files at the Documentation Center. "The other four cards show where the gold is hidden in Berlin, the location of the secret hiding place. But this—" he waved the card back and forth "—this one shows the secret passages that lead to it."

He threw the card on the table below the portrait of Adolf Hitler.

"We must move quickly," Wolfgang said as his enthusiasm returned.

"Now!" was Uwe's reply.

IN THE MERC'S SUITE at the hotel, Barrabas and O'Toole explained the day's events to Nanos and Beck. Brown removed the SS papers from his pockets and flattened them carefully on the coffee table.

"So where is it?" Nanos said eagerly, sitting forward on the couch to look at what Brown was doing.

"Patience, Alex," Brown said. He looked at both sides of each piece of paper. Some he threw aside. Finally he was left with the four SS identity cards. He flipped them over.

"A map of Berlin," he announced, organizing them into a square. "Of Potsdamerplatz."

The map was hastily drawn in ink, the lines faded and almost colorless on the yellowed paper. The Tiergarten and the River Spree were clearly marked, along with the adjacent maze of city streets that had long since disappeared in the Second World War bombings and behind the wall that now divided the one-time capital of the Nazi Reich.

Starting at the top, Brown moved his finger down the center of the map, tracing over the lines. "This is where the wall is today," he explained. "This is Potsdamerplatz, before the war. The empty field on the other side of the wall I showed you today." He circled one area slowly.

"And there's the gold," Nate Beck murmured.

A square in the center of the map near Potsdamerplatz had been drawn with heavier lines.

"I don't believe it," Brown said matter-of-factly. He peered closely at the map again.

"What is it?" Barrabas asked.

Brown shook his head. "It shows the gold is hidden—" he looked up at the mercs, puzzled "—right underneath Hitler's bunker."

The mercs crowded closer around the map.

"What are these numbers?" Barrabas pointed to the spot marked "Reich's Chancellery."

"The bunker—where Hitler committed suicide in 1945—was built under the Chancellery, which was the Nazi version of the White House. But here..." He leaned close, studying the map. "These numbers refer to different levels below the Chancellery. It looks as if the gold is hidden in a deeper level, underneath the bunker itself."

"Then it's simple," Nanos said. "We go in through the Chancellery."

"The Chancellery and the bunker, Alex, are now buried under a field and the field happens to be the main firing zone of the Berlin Wall," O'Toole told the Greek.

"So is that it? Game over?" Nanos asked, looking at the others.

"Wait a minute," Barrabas said. He bent over the map again. "Why does this whole area around the Chancellery have a box drawn around it. What does this say?" He tapped at some more writing.

"There's an insert." Brown said, scanning the German words. "Of course. There were five members of the SS group. There must be a fifth card!" He rummaged through the papers that he had discarded earlier.

"Not there?" Barrabas asked.

Brown shook his head.

"These are subway lines, aren't they?" Nate Beck asked, pointing to the long black lines drawn across Potsdamerplatz. "And steam tunnels. They marked in steam tunnels. Why?"

"That's right," Brown said, following Nate's finger.

There was a moment of silence.

"If the little inset map of this area included the subway and the steam tunnels . . ." Brown began.

"Then that's probably the way in," O'Toole finished.

"Great!" Nanos added. "But without the details, how're we going to know?"

Barrabas spoke. "Nate. Maybe we can construct our own inset." The men looked at the computer wizard from New York.

"I brought the computer," he told them. "Sure. I can tap into the city of Berlin's records and see what I can find."

It took Beck a few minutes to set up his portable computer and plug his modem into the hotel telephone.

"With this," he explained, "my computer can talk to any other main computer line that is hooked into the phone system—as long as I can find the right entry code and break in. That'll take a few minutes, fellas."

While Beck busied himself on the keyboard, Barrabas and O'Toole cleaned up. A bullet had seared its way across Barrabas's left forearm, leaving an ugly gaping wound and a dull ache. It was inconvenient but not incapacitating. O'Toole was in worse shape. A couple of bullets had punched past his chest, deflected by his heavy leather shoulder holster and left him with two bruised, possibly broken ribs. In itself the injury wasn't serious but it made every breath a little painful.

Half an hour later, Beck called to his fellow mercs.

"I'm in. And I've got the engineers' plans for the subways of Berlin."

The other four men crowded around the monitor. Complicated geometric lines danced on the screen as the images changed. Beck's fingers flew along the keyboard, occasionally pausing as he read the monitor.

"The subway line near the bunker hooks into the West Berlin subway system," he stated, looking at Brown.

"That's right," the CIA man answered. "Two of West Berlin's lines run north to south and have to go underneath East Berlin for several kilometers. The trains don't stop after they leave West Berlin. And the stations inside East Berlin have been sealed for twenty years. The platforms are usually patrolled by policemen."

"Well, we're in luck," Beck said, his eyes fixed to the screen. "Because the West Berlin government has the renderings of the underground installations along the subway lines in the Eastern sector. And there it is."

The image changed rapidly several times, then stopped. The men recognized a more complex picture of the map they had looked at earlier.

"What are these?" Barrabas asked, pointing to boxed-in areas filled with diagonal lines near the subway.

Beck pressed a few more command keys. A window formed with a legend explaining the symbols on the diagram.

"Danger zones," he stated flatly. "Locations of suspected ammo dumps left over from the Second World War."

O'Toole whistled. "It's a bloody minefield."

The image on the screen returned to the diagram of the subway line running through Potsdamerplatz.

"Let's zoom in closer," Barrabas suggested.

"Sure." Again Beck pressed a few commands. The image flashed, its edges disappearing as the center grew bigger.

"Now we're getting somewhere," Brown murmured. "That's it. That's the inset we're missing."

The new larger image showed the subways with engineers' markings for electrical conduits and steam tunnels. On the bottom right an ammo dump was marked. Next to it, on the left and barely ten meters away from the subway line, was the foundation of a building. It wasn't labeled, but it was obviously the *Führerbunker.*

"Now, is there a way of getting from the subway tunnel to the bunker?" Beck scrutinized the image on his computer screen. "Nothing's marked. So either there isn't one after all..."

"Or it was sealed years ago, when the bunker was buried," O'Toole added.

"What are these?" Brown asked, pointing to some small lines that appeared to run under the subway tracks on the diagram.

Beck pecked away on the keyboard again. The picture on the screen grew even larger. "A sewer," he said finally. "But it's kind of odd. There's a drainage line leading under the subway tracks. This one is even deeper."

"If the gold is hidden one level under the bunker, it's liable to be deeper than the subway tunnels, too," Brown calculated.

The mercs fell into a momentary silence, watching the computer monitor.

"Follow them," Barrabas suggested.

"The drainage line?" Beck asked.

"Yeah. The deep one. See where it goes."

Beck typed commands into the computer. Once again the image jumped and was replaced by a new diagram showing the same area several hundred feet to the south.

"It doesn't go anywhere," Beck stated. He pressed commands again and the screen showed the area to the north. "Look. it's a dead end there too!"

"It's not a drainage line," Barrabas concluded.

"And it runs within a hundred feet of the bunker," O'Toole pointed out.

"What'll you bet that's it," Nanos said. "That's our way in."

"There's no guarantee," Beck stated.

"Make my day!" Nanos cried boisterously.

"We had ours made several times already," Brown muttered.

"Tom, what time does the subway stop running?" Barrabas asked.

"Stops at 0100. And it starts again just after 0400 hours."

Barrabas looked at his watch. "That gives us an hour to get ready and four hours to get in and get out."

"Have you got a plan in mind, Colonel?" O'Toole asked.

Barrabas leaned over Beck and the computer again. "Show us the general layout again."

Beck typed in the commands. A map of Potsdamerplatz and the area around the wall stretching down to Checkpoint Charlie appeared.

"What do you know about these abandoned subway stations, Tom?" Barrabas asked the CIA man. "Like this one here." He pointed to a spot marked "Leipzigerstrasse" on the computer map.

"There are entrances at street level. Sealed with iron gates at the top and steel doors at the bottom. I don't know how the police get in."

"But we can get in that way. Wait for the last train to go through. Then walk up the tunnels to the abandoned station at Potsdamerplatz."

"Which will put us right smack dab under the middle of the Berlin wall." Liam O'Toole could barely restrain his laughter and winced from his sore ribs.

The other mercs started to laugh.

"What's so funny?" Brown asked.

"Nothing," Beck answered. "Just another routine assignment for the SOBs."

Barrabas checked the mag on his Jati and threw one of the extra guns to Nanos. "Routine," he growled. "But always entertaining."

THE LANDESWEHR KANAL, near the Nazi Documentation Center, was circled with army vehicles, police cars and ambulances. Reporters jostled for information. Heavy body bags were wheeled one by one from the building. Military and civilian police photographed the carnage and scoured the parking lot and the building for clues.

Outside the front doors, Colonel Chillcot of the American Military Police talked to the striking blond woman in the long black leather coat. She was a captain in the dreaded East German Stapo, which gave her a certain immunity in West Berlin. She also had a reputation. Despite her official name, everyone knew her as Ilsa.

After looking at the mess inside the Center and the number of bodies sprawled all over, it was no surprise to Colonel Chillcot that Ilsa was there. Two of her men had been found crushed to death under a ton of books and old files. Dead men can't be questioned, and Ilsa was hardly cooperative.

"As I've told you, Colonel Chillcot," she said smoothly, lighting a cigarette, "I acted on a tip. I came here and found this. My men were attacked by Nazi hooligans that you capitalists allow to run free." She blew out the smoke and blinked. The long red nails that held the cigarette were real. The razor blades had been discreetly removed.

"And how do you suppose that happened?" Chillcot pointed to the bloody thing that had been Dietmar just as the paramedics zipped up the body bag. Chillcot had heard stories of Ilsa's preferred choice of weaponry. He had never believed the stories until now.

"I'm sure I don't know." She puffed on her cigarette, holding the smoke in her mouth and inhaling slowly through her nose. She blew it off to one side, her eyes once again looking Chillcot over, as if she were making a sexual assessment. A big black Russian car pulled through the police lines and slowed behind her. "Excuse me, Colonel." She smiled slightly, tossing her blond hair back.

"There's a helluva mess here for me to clean up," Colonel Chillcot said, eyeing her steadily.

"And I'm sure you'll do a wonderful job." She spun around and walked to the car. The driver closed the rear door after her.

Ilsa sat back and watched the police and ambulance lights flickering blue and red across Colonel Chillcot's face. She looked at the other man in the rear seat of the Russian limo. The *Ministerium* in East Berlin had taken an interest in these matters, and Bruno Kollwitz was very senior in the *Ministerium*.

"We ordered you not to use those...those weapons!" he scolded Ilsa angrily.

Ilsa shrugged, not looking at him. "So?"

Kollwitz sputtered.

Ilsa nailed him with a furious stare. "I am an efficient officer of the Stapo. When I am less than that, you may dismiss me. Meanwhile, my methods are not a matter for discussion."

"What do you intend to do?" Kollwitz asked, his voice suddenly weak, his manner timid. He was a lot more comfortable when he was sitting behind his big mahogany desk at the *Ministerium*. Government officials were the same all over.

"You know as well as I do where they will go next, the American spy and his friends. If they have the map—and I am certain they do—they will try to get the gold."

"It should have been removed years ago," Kollwitz muttered.

"But it wasn't. It's still there. Although..." Ilsa thought for a moment. "Wouldn't it be a wonderful propaganda victory. One that you could take credit for, Bruno. Think of your career."

Suddenly Kollwitz was all ears.

"You have an idea, my dear Ilsa?"

"Would it not be embarrasing for Western powers if their agents—these young Nazis, the CIA spy and his henchmen—were caught red-handed...together?"

"But that would mean revealing the terrible secret!"

"Of course. And using it against the capitalists.

"But how can we make sure it is widely reported in the Western media?"

"We will do something that will shock the world," said Ilsa. "Something that no one can ignore. Let them bring their television cameras and set them up on the lookout platform at Potsdamerplatz." Ilsa leaned forward to the front seat and spoke urgently to the driver. "Use the radio. Have them bring bulldozers to the guardpost at the wall at Potsdamerplatz."

"What?" Kollwitz asked, both excited and worried.

"We will do the unthinkable," Ilsa explained. "We will unseal the Chancellery after forty years and open Hitler's bunker."

18

The streets of East Berlin in the vicinity of Checkpoint Charlie were deserted at midnight. An occasional car drove down from Alexanderplatz to cross the border into the West. The strip along the wall was a brightly lit ribbon running through streets lined with darkened government buildings. On a corner, in the shadows of a doorway, Barrabas waited patiently.

He was dressed in black, a dark jacket hiding the Jati in his shoulder holster. In his pockets he had a flashlight and the Browning HP for backup.

He took out one of the thin cigars that he smoked occasionally, lit it and waited.

Ten minutes later he saw Nanos, Beck and Brown drive through Checkpoint Charlie in the blue Mustang. None of them had the military passes that had allowed O'Toole and Barrabas to pass freely. They had taken a taxi over earlier, bringing their own weapons. In a small leather valise Barrabas carried the two extra Jatis for Nanos and Beck.

The Mustang pulled through the last gate and turned onto Leipzigerstrasse, its headlights sweeping across the road and brushing the toes of Barrabas's boots. It slowed and coasted to a stop at the curb. The door opened.

Barrabas darted across the sidewalk and got in.

Beck was in the back seat. Nanos rode up front with Brown.

"Straight ahead. Another block," Barrabas told them. "Any problems coming through?"

Brown turned around from the driver's seat. "Uh-uh. I guess the last thing they figured I'd do is head back here."

"Or else they're waiting for us up ahead," Nanos cracked. Tom Brown eased the car away from the curb and drove on. Barrabas opened the valise and distributed the Jatis and ammo to Nanos and Beck.

Brown parked again. The subway entrance where he had left O'Toole twenty minutes earlier was several blocks away. The men walked steadily but without discernible haste until they came to the place. A low wrought-iron grille surrounded some steps at the street corner. The steps led down.

"Wait here," Barrabas ordered. He stepped over the grill and descended. O'Toole waited for him at the bottom, tamping a detonator wire into the plastic explosives that had been pressed between the two metal doors.

"Finished?" Barrabas asked.

"Just." The demolitions expert wiped his hands and unrolled a small spool of wire. "I used a minimum amount of explosive so it will be quiet. But those doors are pretty thick."

They returned up the steps to street level, with O'Toole uncoiling the wire. The mercs waited around the corner of the building.

"What happens if someone hears this?" Nanos asked.

"We might get as far as the car," Brown whispered. "But not much farther."

Far down the street, headlights appeared.

"Do it, O'Toole!" Barrabas ordered.

The sargeant squeezed the small electrical detonator with his hand.

The sidewalk vibrated slightly, and the low sound of soft thunder emanated from the sealed subway entrance. A small cloud of dust floated up to the street.

"Wait," Barrabas said.

The car bore down on them, but passed, its red taillights growing small until it disappeared around the corner toward Checkpoint Charlie.

"Let's go for it!" Barrabas ran across the sidewalk and descended the steps. The explosion had blown the locks on the huge metal doors.

Barrabas kept one hand on his Jati and held his flashlight with the other. He slipped through the doors into total darkness, stopped and flicked the flashlight on and off—enough to tell him he had about ten feet to go to another set of stairs that led farther down. The other mercs crowded in the broken doors behind him.

The stairs led down another twenty feet below street level. They were wet and littered with bits of broken tile.

"Nanos, give us some light from the rear," Barrabas ordered.

He extinguished his flashlight when the Greek put his on. The shadows of the five men fell down the steps ahead of them.

The mercs fanned out in a line along the steps and descended. There was no resistance. At the bottom, abandoned turnstiles indicated the way to the platform of the deserted underground station.

As they approached the last steps that would take them to the platform, a very faint light glowed against the peeling walls. Barrabas stood at the top of the stairs.

Below, on the platform, three policemen were walking quickly toward the steps. One gave orders to the other two. Their submachine guns were up and ready.

Barrabas snapped his fingers at Nanos, Beck and Brown, motioning them to stand in the darkness at the side of the stairwell. He and O'Toole pushed against the other wall. Barrabas took the HP from his pocket and held it by the barrel.

They heard the sound of footsteps on the gritty stairs.

Three guards appeared at the top.

Barrabas swung at the leader and connected. The handle of the HP slammed into the base of the man's cranium. He grunted painfully before the lights went out. Barrabas caught the man as he fell into unconsciousness.

Beside him, O'Toole was dragging the second man back with his hand over his mouth. Nanos had knocked the third man out. Brown helped him lower the body. Beck jumped to help O'Toole. He slammed his Jati into the guard's temple. "Shut up!" he cried. If the policeman didn't understand English, he understood the tone of voice. Dead serious. He stopped struggling.

Suddenly Barrabas was there, grabbing the man's handcuffs from his belt and slipping them over the policeman's wrists.

"Gibt es noch Polizei?" Brown demanded from the frightened policeman, jerking his head toward the subway platform.

"Ja. Zwei."

"There are two more policemen down there," the CIA man told the others.

"Brown, Beck, tie them and gag them," Barrabas ordered. "O'Toole and Nanos, follow me."

The three mercs went down the steps and stood at the bottom looking along the dimly lit platform. The filthy floor was littered with broken tiles. Paint peeled from the ceiling. Wooden benches had rotted into collapse after twenty years' disuse. In the center of the platform, fifty feet away, was a derelict newsstand covered with faded advertising boards. There was no sign of the two policemen.

Running lightly along the platform, they came to the old newsstand and just as one of the policemen came around the corner, Barrabas swung the barrel of the Jati flat into the man's stomach. With a loud grunt, the man doubled over. Ten feet away, the colonel saw the shocked face of the second guard.

"Take care of it," Barrabas told Nanos and O'Toole. The second policeman turned to run. Barrabas sprinted past the newsstand after him.

The distance between him and the fleeing guard closed quickly. The man reached the stairs at the far end of the platform. He grabbed a handgun from his holster and turned, holding it in both hands and aiming it at Barrabas.

The merc threw himself forward and shouldered the policeman before he got the shot off. The German guard fell back on the stairs, with Barrabas's steel grip on the wrist of the hand that held the gun. He twisted. The gun dropped. Barrabas slugged him in the face. He struck again, knuckling into the soft spot of his temple. The guard's eyes closed. He slipped into unconsciousness.

Quickly Barrabas flipped the body over, found the handcuffs and fastened the man's hands. Nanos came up behind him.

"What time is it?" Barrabas snapped.

"Zero hour fifty," the Greek told him. O'Toole, Nate and Brown joined them on the platform.

Far down the line they heard the distant rumble of the last subway train from West Berlin. The headlight from the front of the train pierced the darkness of the station.

"Where did you put the other guard?" Barrabas asked.

"Out of sight in that old newsstand," Brown said, as Beck and Nanos dragged the last unconscious man up the steps.

"That's the last train of the night," Barrabas said. "As soon as it's through, we go down the tracks to the next station, Potsdamerplatz. We take out the guards there the same way."

"It'd be a lot faster just to..." Nanos held up his SMG.

"Uh-uh," Barrabas said. "In the world of mercenaries and spies, it's dog eat dog. But these buggers are innocent. They have wives and kids. So we do it clean."

The light from the subway train grew brighter. The SOBs drew back from sight. The noise of the wheels on their metal rails drowned out the last of Barrabas's words.

THE LAST TRAIN SLOWED as it left the subway station on the west side of the Berlin wall and crossed into the east.

Uwe and Wolfgang stood at the end of the final car, surveying the other passengers. An old drunk nodded off to sleep, his body rocking with the movement of the train. Toward the front of the car, a young couple were engrossed in each other.

"We must make sure no one sees us," Uwe said.

"This would be easiest." Wolfgang patted the metal frame of the Schmeisser hidden under his long coat.

"*Nein*, that is not necessary," Uwe said. "The bodies will be found too soon."

The train picked up speed in the tunnel, then slowed again as it approached the abandoned station at Leipzigerstrasse. Through the windows of the car they could make out the dilapidated platform and the abandoned newsstand.

"Where are the policemen?" Wolfgang demanded.

"They are there," Uwe replied. "Somewhere."

"But they always patrol the platform. I see no one."

"They are out of sight!" Uwe replied with annoyance. "Besides, these policemen we do not have to worry about. It is the ones at the Potsdamerplatz station."

"Those we kill."

Uwe nodded. "They are enemies of the Reich."

Once again the train picked up speed as it left the Leipzigerstrasse station and headed for Potdamerplatz. Uwe glanced at the passengers. The drunk was still asleep. The young couple were making out.

He opened the door at the end of the car half a foot.

"Go!" he whispered urgently. Wolfgang slipped through and stood on the bumper of the car. Uwe took one last look. The train was slowing as it entered the next station. He slipped through, closing the door behind him. As the train entered Potsdamerplatz station, Uwe and Wolfgang dropped off the end of the car onto the tracks.

They waited in the tunnel as the train disappeared through the station. Three policemen stood on the platform, watching it grow small in the far tunnel.

"Come!" Uwe ordered.

The two neo-Nazi storm troopers ran down the tracks, keeping their heads below the level of the platform until they were only a few feet from the policemen.

Uwe straightened, swinging his silenced Schmeisser in an arc and pressed the trigger on full-auto. Wolfgang followed his lead. The policemen's faces registered surprise as the bullets tore through their bodies. They crumpled into a bloody pile. A long plume of blood jetted out from underneath and sluiced over the edge of the platform.

"Was ist los!" an alarmed voice called from farther down the station.

Uwe and Wolfgang ducked under the platform again and raced down the tracks.

Two more policemen swung around a deserted kiosk.

The two German youths jumped up, their Schmeissers blasting. Both policemen took it in the face. They slammed into each other and tumbled over. The sound of running feet alerted Uwe to the last policeman, fleeing in panic for cover on the opposite tracks.

He swung his Schmeisser and striped bullets down the man's back. The gaurd's momentum carried him forward. He disappeared over the edge. Uwe hopped onto the platform and ran across. He looked down at the bloody body sprawled on the tracks.

The opposition had been eliminated.

Wolfgang leaned over two of the dead policemen. He had their shirts stripped back. With the blade of a sharp knife, he carved bloody swastikas into their chests.

"We have no time for that," Uwe whispered furiously. "Come! The gold awaits us!"

Wolfgang stood, wiping the knife on his pants before putting it away.

"For the fatherland!" he proclaimed.

"Sieg heil," Uwe answered. They jumped onto the tracks. The subway tunnel beckoned like a mouth yawning into darkness and luring them to Nazi gold.

BARRABAS AND HIS SOLDIERS ran through the subway tunnel. The tiny circle of light far ahead marked the Potsdamerplatz station. As it grew bigger, Barrabas told his men to slow their pace and proceed quietly.

He crept toward the opening, scanning the subway platform as it came into view. There was no sign of any policemen.

"Maybe they go off duty after the last train goes through," O'Toole whispered.

Maybe, thought Barrabas. But it didn't seem likely.

When they got to the edge of the tunnel, the question was answered. A pile of bodies lay on the station platform. Blood dripped slowly onto the tracks.

They proceeded cautiously, listening for noise and watching for movement. Finally the men drew abreast of the three bodies. The bloody swastikas were clearly visible on the dead men's chests.

"The Nazis," Tom Brown said when he saw the hack job. "They're here, too."

"Butchering bastards," Nate Beck swore.

"Nanos, O'Toole, check the tracks on the other side of the platform," Barrabas ordered. The two men leaped up and crossed over.

"They probably have the inset map," Brown said to Barrabas. "They're ahead of us down the tunnel."

The colonel nodded, feeling a knot of tension tighten in his gut. They were boxed in underground, and he hated it, hated the feeling of growing danger and the sense that there was no way out. He had never liked urban warfare. He'd takc the jungle anytime.

"We've come too far to back out now. Besides, there's no way I'm letting these Nazi punks get their hands on that gold."

Nanos and O'Toole slid back onto the tracks.

"There's no sign of the Nazis," O'Toole reported. "But there are three more bodies farther along the platform."

"Then they finished here," Barrabas said. "They've gone on to the bunker." He looked squarely from man to man. "You all know what's going on here. Any one want to back out before we go in deeper?"

"Hell, Colonel. How can we? Next subway train doesn't come till four this morning!" Nanos half-smiled when he said it.

The whole mission was a bad joke.

UWE AND WOLFGANG EMERGED from their hiding place below the platform on the other side of the tracks and watched until the SOBs were out of sight in the tunnel ahead.

"Who are these men?" Wolfgang asked.

"I do not know," said Uwe.

"Unless we kill them immediately, they will find the way to the gold."

"Let them. Once they have found the way for us, we can liquidate them." Uwe looked at his watch. "Ten minutes. Then we will pursue."

AT THE GUARD TOWER along the wall at Potsdamerplatz, klieg lights carved up the night along the minefields and vehicle barricades. On the western side of the wall, journalists and reporters crowded onto the platform that looked into East Berlin. Television cameras and technicians were positioned in buckets on high-ladder trucks.

On the eastern side Bruno Kollwitz stood anxiously beside Ilsa, watching two giant bulldozers roll down from a flatbed truck. Army trucks lined the road, and young soldiers jumped from the tailgates, waiting at attention for their orders.

"I hope you are right," Kollwitz said. He still hadn't made up his mind whether this would advance his career or lock him forever in some low-level clerical job in a remote labor camp.

Ilsa looked at him, not concealing her dislike. "It is too late to back out now, Bruno. Our audience is eager and waiting." She looked across the field at the high concrete wall and the reporters scrambling on the western side. "They are curious to know what all this commotion is about."

Kollwitz nodded doubtfully. "I hope you are right."

"We will find out sooner or later," Ilsa said with grim certainty.

The giant bulldozers rolled along the road and through the high steel fence. Soldiers cordoned off the low grassy hill that lay on the edge of the minefield that fronted the Wall. The first bulldozer lowered its shovel and dug at the ground, tearing away the sod and exposing chunks of stone and rubble. The driver backed up, dumped the debris and took another run at the hill. This time, the corner of a stone wall was revealed. The second bulldozer tackled the small hill from the other side.

Soldiers in fatigues waited with shovels, while their officers circled the hill on foot, unrolling blueprints and tattered old maps.

"How long will it take?" Kollwitz asked.

"Only a few minutes," Ilsa said. "And for the first time in four decades, the world will see the inside of Hitler's bunker."

19

The SOBs marched along the tracks of the subway tunnel. The blinding darkness made their hearing more accute. Barrabas listened to the soft sound of his soldiers' footsteps and the slow drip of water from above. Far ahead, an opening of light marked another deserted subway station on the north side of Potsdamerplatz. The Nazis were nowhere in sight.

Barrabas felt a hand on his shoulder. It was Nate Beck. He flicked on his light and indicated a three-foot recess in the stone wall. The bottom was covered by an old iron grate.

"That's it," Beck whispered.

Nanos and Beck each took a corner and lifted. At first it didn't move. The men strained against decades of rust and dirt. Nanos's end came up quickly, then Beck's. Brown and Barrabas added their strength. The grate came free, jerking suddenly from its frame. The mercs pushed it sideways and leaned it against the wall. Barrabas shone his light into the opening.

A concrete stairway led down. The bottom was covered with a foot of muck. A rat, blinded by the flashlight, squeaked in panic and jumped farther back into the darkness of the tunnel.

"Ready?" Barrabas looked at the mercs and Brown. The men nodded. The colonel descended, his boots sinking into the muck at the bottom of the stairs. His flashlight flickered over metal cases that lined the walls. The mercs crowded down the steps behind their leader.

"Shit," Barrabas muttered.

"What is it?" O'Toole asked.

"Those crates. They've been sitting there since the Second World War. They're marked 'high explosives.'"

"Ammunition," said Beck, shining his flashlight over the faded stenciled letters on the rusting metal cases.

"For the resistance that never came," said Brown.

O'Toole nodded. "And for forty years, extremely volatile. The slightest vibration at the wrong time could set it off."

Suddenly the mercs stopped moving and stood very still. There was a cold creepy chill about the place that had no scientific explanation.

Barrabas walked farther into the darkness, slowly passing the ammo cases. Each footstep was an effort. The muck swallowed his boots and held them down. Twenty feet farther along, three short steps led to a barred gate. Flakes of rust peeled from the iron. Barrabas tapped it with the barrel of his Jati. The rusty lock crumbled and fell. The gate swung slowly open with a long wrenching shriek.

Another long tunnel led upward. Halfway along it, the muck ended and the floor was dry. One side was piled high with more ammo cases stamped with swastikas.

"Hitler's last stand," Brown said behind him. "No human being has set foot in here in forty years."

"Longer," O'Toole muttered. "The Nazis weren't human."

Barrabas swept the path ahead of him with his light. His other hand clenched the Jati, tightening on the trigger. What were they armed against, he asked himself. Ghosts?

He stopped. His flashlight picked out a skeleton grinning up at him from the floor. The Nazi uniform rotted onto the bones and the visored officer's hat perched on the skull were grim reminders of the fate of the thousand-year Reich.

Abruptly the tunnel ended. Barrabas's light emptied into a great dark space. He shone the beam down. It traveled along the floor until it caught the edge of a round wooden crate. A barrel. He shone the beam around the room and the other mercs came up behind him.

The room was about forty feet long and almost as wide. The walls were piled high with ammo cases. The room was filled with rows of wooden barrels.

Tom Brown pushed into the room. "The gold!" he said. "The..." He stopped. He shone his light into one of the barrels. It glittered and sparkled on dark yellow metal.

Barrabas came down the steps with the SOBs behind him. The gold was everywhere, little flakes and nuggets were piled high in the barrels and in mounds on the floor.

"What the hell?" O'Toole said in surprise. "It's not—"

"Yeah. It's not gold bars or coins. What is it?" Nanos said slowly.

Tom Brown lifted a handful of little pieces of gold from one of the barrels. It was old and dull. He held the pieces in the palm of his hand.

"Fillings," said Barrabas. "From human teeth. Tons of them. A hundred million dollars' worth."

"Colonel," Beck shone his light on the side of one of the barrels. Even after forty years the stencilled markings were still legible. It read "Auschwitz."

Brown dropped the tiny chunks of gold and fell to his knees. He gagged in uncontrollable spasms.

Overhead a sound like thunder reverberated through the bunker's ceiling. The men listened. Barrabas looked at O'Toole, the SOBs demo expert.

His words were dry in his throat. "They're digging us up!"

THE BRIGHT YOUNG East German lieutenant snapped his heels together and saluted.

"They have uncovered the entrance, Captain."

The bulldozer pulled back from the deep excavation of underground walls. The remains of broken steps led down into the ground. A team of soldiers carrying shovels ran from rows of men standing at attention to tackle the dirt and debris that clogged the entrance to Hitler's bunker.

"Very good," Ilsa said, motioning to Kollwitz and walked past the young lieutenant. "Will you be the first to go down, Bruno?" The she-wolf's offer was generous. "It could make your career." She smiled. She was teasing.

"I suggest a platoon of heavily armed men," Kollwitz replied testily.

Ilsa stretched her arm and snapped her fingers. Instantly thirty men, padded in bulletproof vests, helmeted and heavy with automatic rifles double-timed past Ilsa and the man from the *Ministerium*. They took up positions in a line behind the bulldozer.

"I am still uncomfortable about the gold," said Kollwitz. "It was left there after the war because..."

"But it is not our people who are after it. It is the capitalist warmongers. If there is guilt about the origins of the gold, let it be their guilt, not ours." Ilsa stepped nearer the pit."You may be afraid, dear Bruno, but I shall go in there with my men and see for myself the faces of these vermin." From her pocket she removed the soft leather pouch. Inside it, her razors rattled.

"Not those!" Kollwitz said, aghast. "Not here, in front of those Western TV cameras!"

There was noise from the bottom of the excavation. "We're through!" a soldier shouted.

Ilsa waved the pouch of deadly razors in Kollwitz's face, snickered and walked past him.

UWE AND WOLFGANG CROUCHED in the narrow passageway near the skeletal remains of the dead Nazi. They watched the weaving flashlight beams of the SOBs emanating from the gold room ahead.

Wide-eyed with fear and awe, Uwe reached out to finger the blackened medals hanging from the skeleton's rotted uniform. His fingers barely brushed it when the bones rolled and the skeleton broke in two. The visored helmet fell, exposing a toothy smile. The skull clattered along the floor. Wolfgang jumped back and aimed his Schmeisser.

"Wait!" Uwe put his hand up.

They listened.

A rumbling overhead grew to a deafening boom. Wolfgang gulped. Uwe's eyes shone like white slits in the darkness. He stared at the trembling ceiling.

"The gods are with us! Thor! Siegfried! They ride their war chariots in battle at our sides. We are invincible!"

"Uwe! Uwe!" Wolfgang whispered madly. His berserk leader seemed not to hear. "Look at me!" Wolfgang cried, grabbing Uwe's shirt and shaking him.

Uwe stared through him. With his forearm he pushed the insignificant Wolfgang aside. His eyes shone across the darkness as he stared ahead at the entrance to the gold room. He raised his Schmeisser firmly in both hands and started walking.

"O'TOOLE, HOW MUCH PLASTIC have you got left?" Barrabas snapped at his second in command.

The Irish-American merc shot his eyes quickly along the rows of metal ammunition boxes.

"Enough to set this stuff off and blow Hitler's bunker straight to hell."

"Wire it!" Barrabas ordered.

Tom Brown stood shakily nearby. He fumbled at his inside breast pocket for his silver flask and gulped back a mouthful of vodka. The CIA spy jerked his head as the liquid burned its way down.

"I think I'll pass on this fortune in gold," he told Barrabas.

The underground room shook with the closer rumbling of heavy machinery. There was an abrupt silence. The mercs listened to a strange scuffling sound along one wall.

"They're using shovels," Nanos said.

Nate Beck worked quickly, stringing a long thin filament along the side of the room to the tunnel entrance. At the far end O'Toole carefully pressed the last of his plastic along the edge of the row of ammo cases.

"Come on, let's get out of here," Barrabas said. Any minute someone or something was going to crash through the pile of debris that blocked the entrance.

"Brown! Let's go! Alex!" He coverd the entrance with his Jati, moving from foot to foot as he directed his men out of the hell hole. O'Toole pressed the detonator cord carefully into the plastics.

Booooom!

The room shook violently. Something very big pounded against the walls of the bunker. An avalanche of earth and debris crashed in the entrance, knocking ammo cases onto the floor.

"Colonel, with all this commotion, this old ammo is going to go off and blow us to bits," O'Toole shouted.

The mercs ran for the tunnel as chunks of cement fell from the ceiling, crashing onto the casks of Auschwitz gold. The wall of the bunker split. Great boulders of cement bound by steel reinforcement rods pushed inward. The mammoth blade of a bulldozer gleamed dully amid the earth and debris. With a wretching grind, it backed up and pounded forward again, straining against tons of concrete. The steel bars bent and snapped as the room moved in. Debris rolled and fell, exposing the spotlit night outside. The dozer backed off and a line of armed Stapo troopers ran into the gap.

Suddenly, from the tunnel that led back to the subway, the mercs heard harsh German words shouted in panic. Uwe lurched stiffly through the entrance to the gold room, pressing the trigger of his Schmeisser.

Full-auto.

Nine-millimeter lead pounded from the Schmeisser mag into the Stapo's bulletproof vests. One Stapo trooper took it in the face. His scream was short. The others abandoned their dead brother as they scrambled out of the line of fire.

Caught right in the middle in the brief moment of confusion, the mercs flattened themselves on the floor as the Stapo returned fire. Bullets chunked into barrels of gold and chipped at the concrete bunker.

"Out!" Barrabas shouted at his soldiers through the din. He grabbed the roll of detonator wire from Nate Beck. "Get out!" he ordered.

Uwe walked past the mercs deeper into the underground room, still firing. Wolfgang bounded after him. East German soldiers swung a portable spotlight into place. Light bobbed through the bunker as they attempted to steady it. A steady stream of empty cartridge shells popped from Uwe's Schmeisser as he autofired at the police and the bulldozer. Then nothing.

His mag was out.

Wolfgang threw himself at his lost leader.

The two men crashed to the floor.

"Now!" Barrabas shouted.

Brown and the mercs jumped from the floor and ducked into the passageway to escape. The spotlight beam flooded into the bunker. Stapo bullets began anew their chorus of autodeath.

Barrabas held the Jati in his left hand and spun out the roll of detonator wire as he ran backward down the corridor. The other mercs raced ahead. Brown tripped and sprawled over the broken skeleton in the tunnel, and Nanos and O'Toole, leaning as they sped through, grabbed him, pulled him to his feet and ran on.

At the stairs that led up to the subway platform, Beck took his wristwatch from his arm and pried the crystal off the face. Working quickly and with the utmost calm, he attached wires from the detonator to the little hands.

"Keep going," he told the other mercs, jerking his head at the stairs.

They rushed past him just as Barrabas arrived. He handed Nate the end of the detonator wire.

"How long?"

"A minute."

"That long?" Beck adjusted the hands on the watch face and set it on the steps.

"We need the time. When all this Nazi ammo blows, it's going to clean out a big chunk of Berlin."

Nate attached the wires from the watch to the detonator with smooth precision.

"Done."

The sounds of ripping autofire carried from the inner hellhole of Hitler's bunker. Barrabas and Beck leaped up the steps and ran into the subway tunnel.

ILSA STOOD IN THE BULLDOZED EARTH, watching as the men shone the spotlight into the gaping hole that led into the underground bunker.

"Please, I beg of you," Bruno Kollwitz pleaded. "Put that terrible weapon away. You have been forbidden..." He looked fearfully at the long razors that Ilsa attached to each of her fingers. Defiant, she held one hand at eye level and fanned the sharp, thin metal slivers, clicking them together.

"Out of my way!" She stepped past him. Below, soldiers were firing into the gold room.

"Not yet!" Kollwitz cried, "Wait for your men to eliminate the opposition."

The blond Stapo mistress turned and eyed him coldly. "When I get there, they will have accomplished that."

Slowly and proudly, Ilsa descended, the hands of death swinging languorously at her side.

WOLFGANG HELD UWE on the floor, straining against his leader's resistance. The autofire from the East German troopers stopped. The single beam of the spotlight moved slowly through the bunker, searching them out.

"Stop, Uwe! Stop! Be calm!" Wolfgang urged. "Or we are dead men."

Uwe relaxed. He moaned and rolled his head back and forth.

"I will get us out of here, Uwe," Wolfgang promised. He raised himself and crouched behind one of the barrels of gold.

"Bitte!" he called. "I am unarmed." He grabbed his Schmeisser and threw it at the light. Time to surrender. "See! That is my rifle!" He raised his arms. His hands appeared above the top of the barrel. No one fired. He started up, slowly, wincing against the light and the half-expected volley of submachinegun fire that would cut him down.

There was silence. He stood.

The light moved, and a single figure was silhouetted in the beam.

"Is there only you?" It was a woman's voice, amused, teasing.

"*Nein*, there is one more."

"Bring him out," the sultry voice coaxed.

Wolfgang bent slowly and grabbed Uwe by his collar. The blond athlete came to his feet. Wolfgang looked at him. It was written as clear as daylight in the young Nazi's eyes. Uwe wasn't mad at all. He was over his head in trouble and scared shitless. He whimpered and sniffed like a little boy, lost and far away from home.

"Come closer." The woman was calling to them. Wolfgang saw her approaching, the bright beam of the light outlining the curve of her waist, the hang of the long leather coat, the long hair swept back over her shoulders. She raised her arms.

Wolfgang screamed. Words shrieked inside him, when he saw her hands—wake up, wake up, it could only be a nightmare.

Ilsa swung her arms vertically, slicing Wolfgang from crotch to forehead. He split open like a garden hose bursting blood. His last shriek died in an inarticulate gargle.

Ilsa's attention was already elsewhere. She looked at Uwe.

"Come to me, little man," she beckoned, curling a finger to draw him near.

The second hand on Nate Beck's watch hit zero. Virtually instantaneously, a small electric spark traveled along a length of wire to the gold room.

BARRABAS RACED THROUGH THE DARK with Nate Beck beside him. Both men ran flat out, legs pumping, like thoroughbreds hot on the finish line. The distance along the silvery rails to the other mercs narrowed. The light from the abandoned station at Potsdamerplatz grew brighter. In his head, Barrabas ticked off the seconds with the expertise of a trained combat soldier.

Time was running out.

Barrabas pushed harder. With an immense effort of will, Beck paced himself beside the colonel. The plastics exploded just as they caught up to O'Toole and Nanos.

The station shook violently and echoed with a thundering boom. Explosion followed explosion, each one louder than the one before. The subway rails bucked. Heavy chunks of tile and concrete crashed from overhead. Another loud explosion boomed up the tunnel as the chain reaction began. The explosions ripped along the weapons depot and rifle caches around the buried bunker.

O'Toole was lagging. He dropped back, his face white with pain. His two broken ribs tore at his side.

"I can't," he gulped heavily as Barrabas caught up to him, "breath enough..."

"Hang on!" the colonel shouted over the deafening thunder of the explosions. Nanos ran back as Barrabas draped the Irishman's arm around his shoulder. The Greek caught the other side.

The explosions ripped through the ground as the mercs crossed the abandoned station into the darkened tunnel that led to Leipzigerstrasse. Brown dropped back to relieve Barrabas. The colonel and Beck ran along the platform onto the steps, where the policemen remained bound and gagged.

"It's still clear!" Barrabas shouted. He headed for street level.

The night outside was raw with the noise of sirens and exploding ammo dumps. Half a klick away, great clouds of dirt and black smoke blew into the air behind the guard tower at Potsdamerplatz. A series of explosions suddenly blew in a rapid line down the wall.

"The ammo dumps have set off the East German wall defences—the mines set to prevent people from escaping."

"Funny you should mention it..." Nate began. Brown and Nanos boosted O'Toole up the steps. The ex-sargeant protested and pulled away. His face winced as pain rippled through his side again, but he was too proud to take any more help.

"How're we escaping?" Beck finished.

A siren shrilled above the general noise. Then another. Far down Leipzigerstrasse headlights approached.

"They're coming for us," Barrabas told them.

"We can still get out," Brown shouted. "In the car."

Barrabas looked at him. "You mean..."

"Unless you can think of a better way," said Brown.

BY THE TIME THE MERCS REACHED Brown's car, half-a-dozen East German police vehicles were hot on their heels. Brown screeched away from the curb just as the first car arrived. He floored it. The Mustang engine roared to full power, instantly distancing them from their pursuers.

Barrabas looked at Brown. The man was driving like a bat bent on a return to hell. The car responded superbly. The night air was filled with the sirens of the hunter cars behind them.

"You seriously think it'll work?" Barrabas yelled at Brown. The spy didn't answer. The car screeched around a corner, throwing Barrabas against the door. In the back seat, Beck landed across Nanos and O'Toole. The Irishman gripped his painful ribs to protect them from the crush. Police cars fishtailed around the corner in hot pursuit. Straight ahead, at the end of the street, was a five-level parking garage.

Brown looked quickly at Barrabas as the car picked up speed again.

"No!" he shouted.

It was the answer Barrabas had expected.

Brown hit the front entrance of the garage at a speed verging on a hundred miles per hour. The wooden rail at the turnstile blew into splinters. The car soared through the first level. Brown steered sharply left and spun the Mustang in a semicircle up an incline to the second. The car screeched and the mercs fell from side to side as Brown drove along the straightaways and up the curving ramps to the top.

They hit the roof.

The skyline of West Berlin lay ahead of them, the lights along the downtown Kurfürstendamm gleaming like a hooker's rhinestones.

Brown pressed the accelerator to the floor. The Mustang flew across the top parking level and crashed through the iron rails at the end.

For a moment they were airborne. The transmission screamed as the tires spun in nothing. As the descent began, Brown released the gas pedal and slammed on the brakes.

The car tilted forward slightly as it fell. It sailed on an angle to the peaked roof of the adjacent building, coming down on the other side. Its underside scraped the roof, showering sparks as they roared down the incline. Below there was a street, barbed wire lining a narrow stretch of minefield and then the Wall. On the other side, in West Berlin, a muddy canal flowed toward the river.

The wheels of the Mustang spun shingles off the roof as the car slowed. They left the roof forty feet above the ground.

"Whooopeeee!" Brown shrieked like a rodeo cowboy. He had one arm on the wheel and waved the other in the air.

On the ground East German border guards grabbed for their rifles. Muzzle-flashes exploded orange below them and bullets arced through the sky. To the north, occasional explosions from buried ammo dumps still blew, and billowing flames lit the night. The city screamed with sirens like a battle station under attack.

The Mustang flew over the minefield, dropping steadily. The front end barely cleared the wall. The murky waters of the canal came up to meet them in a rush of cold, total darkness.

EPILOGUE

Barrabas folded the newspaper and placed it on the table. He drew a thin cigar from his pocket and lit it. The street was lined with outdoor cafés, and by ten o'clock in the morning they were half full. He watched the busy street traffic curl around the walls of a ruined church.

"May I?" It was Tom Brown. His hand rested on the back of a chair.

"Be my guest."

The American spy sat. "The papers have had a field day."

Barrabas nodded. "A terrorist massacre at the Nazi Documentation Center, old Second World War ammo dumps going off in East Berlin and strange stories of a flying car that authorities claim to know nothing about."

"Yeah. All incidents on the same night and no connection between any of them," Brown concluded the news coverage he'd also read in the morning papers.

"Some small journalist will figure something out and come up with a conspiracy theory."

"And no one will believe it, either," said Brown. "No mention of a band of brave Americans in the papers was there?"

"That's the way it usually is. If we start getting publicity, we've done something wrong. Are you sorry about the car?'' The Mustang had been abandoned at the bottom of the canal.

''It was a noble retirement.'' The spy stretched and smiled. ''Oh, I forgot.'' He pulled a small blackened disk from his pocket, and handed it to Barrabas. A scratch on it glinted.

''Gold,'' said Barrabas. It was a coin. No, a medal. With an enamel swastika set in it.

''I grabbed it from the uniform on the skeleton in the tunnel.'' Brown explained. ''Yeah, it's gold. But look.'' He took the medal from Barrabas and turned it over. The owner's initials were engraved on the back. ''A.H.''

''Wonder who that was?'' Brown said casually. He pegged the medal into the street. A perfect throw. It disappeared down the grate of a storm sewer.

''Doesn't matter now, does it?'' said Barrabas.

''Colonel!'' O'Toole's voice boomed in greeting and the tall red-haired man pulled out a chair.

''Where are Nanos and Beck?'' Barrabas asked, turning around.

O'Toole pointed to the far end of the café. The two mercs were inviting themselves to sit down with a couple of lovely *Fräuleins.* ''They didn't even make it across the room. What now, Colonel? I mean, what are your plans?''

Barrabas didn't answer at first. He watched the foot traffic on the sidewalk. ''Leave Europe,'' he said. ''Europe stinks—dying cultures and old ideas and everyone fighting for it all. Maggots swarming on a corpse called history. That's why I love the United States. We have as many people there as live in Europe and sure, we have problems; but at least we're not at each other's throats all the time.''

O'Toole laughed. "Don't be too hard on Europe, Colonel. I just talked to Susy. We're going to continue our honeymoon in Ireland. It's her homeland, too." He looked away, a little embarrassed. Slowly he spoke again. "I guess the last day or so took your mind off things."

"Uh-huh." His memories of Amsterdam and Erika seemed like they belonged to someone else, to some other era. "What about you?"

O'Toole was startled by the question. He had just had the time of his life, and all thoughts of his new wife and the interrupted honeymoon had been on hold.

Barrabas continued. "Liam, you said we had to talk at the end of this mission."

"Why sure, Colonel," O'Toole said with difficulty.

"But not until after the rest of your vacation with Susy, okay? That way, you'll know for sure what you want. No doubts. No second thoughts. All right?"

O'Toole looked relieved. He nodded.

Barrabas turned to Tom Brown. "Are you disappointed about the gold?"

Brown laughed. "All that glitters is not..." He shrugged, momentarily serious. "I have my life. My health. How can I not be eternally happy? Maybe if people were satisfied with simple things, there'd be no wars. But then we'd be out of jobs, wouldn't we, Nile?"

Barrabas shook his head slowly and thoughtfully. "There'll always be work for the likes of us, Tom." He stuck his cigar between his teeth and flashed a big toothy smile at his two friends. "Always, for the likes of us!"